THE SCALES ARE OUT OF BALANCE

EPISODE 2

I0459559

JIM JOHNSON

AUTHOR OF RANGER OF MAYAT

www.PISTOLSANDPYRAMIDS.com

ISBN-13: 978-0692639306 (Ineti Press)
ISBN-10: 0692639306

Cover design and print layout by Kevin G. Summers
(www.happycatstudios.com)
Editing by Erica Satifka (www.ericasatifka.com)
Illustrations by James Hale (fantagor72@gmail.com)

We'd love to hear from you! Please send letters and/or postcards of interesting places you've visited to:

INETI PRESS

2308 Mt. Vernon Ave., Ste #325
Alexandria, VA 22301

www.INETIPRESS.com

FOR MOM AND DAD

ILLUSTRATIONS

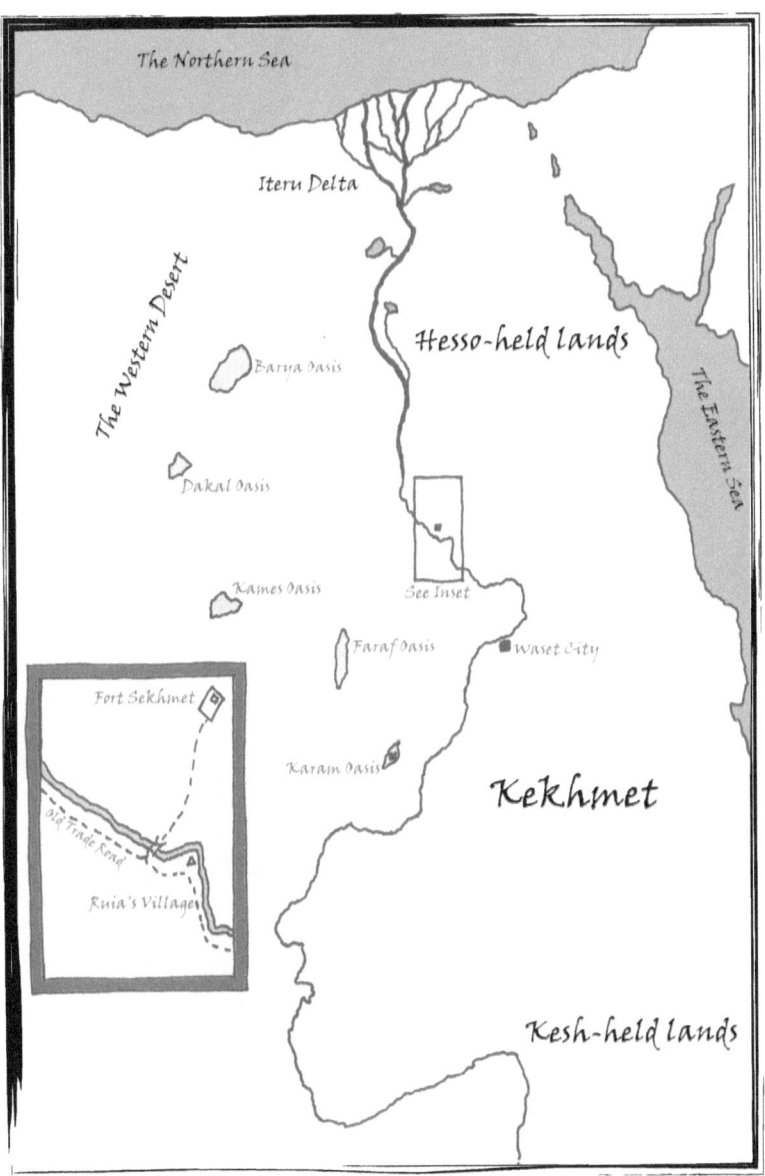

FLIGHT TO THE FORT

A HARSH SHAKING ROUSED Tjety out of his stupor. His fitful vision of a massive sand dragon tearing deep into his body and *ba* abruptly came to a halt. For a moment, he thought he was back in that rocky den chasing down Meret, getting buried in an earthquake, but then his weary senses filtered out his name being repeated, over and over.

"Tjety! Come on, you water-skimmer! Wake up!"

He cracked open crusty eyes and focused on the girl who'd helped save his life and those of her fellow villagers. "Ruia?" He saw the consternation in her expression and pushed himself upright, feeling a twinge of pain from his shot-up arm. "What's wrong?"

Ruia knelt next to him and snorted. "What's

wrong, he says. Other than everything we're dealing with? Things are just fine, sand-dancer."

Tjety pushed himself up into a sitting position, the blanket he'd appropriated from a dead bandit sloughing to the ground. He adjusted the sling around his wounded arm and winced as the motion generated a fresh spear of pain. "What time is it?"

She shrugged. "Morning, yet. Maybe an hour past sunrise."

He stared at her, blinking grit out of his eyes. "Ruia, that other night, the one where you escaped the bandits and went running, the night before you found me...did you feel an earthquake?"

Ruia stared at him with confusion plain in her eyes. "Earthquake? No. I don't remember anything like that." She stared away. "Of course, so much was happening, but...I'm sure I would have remembered." She focused on him again. "Why?"

He met her glance and then looked away. "By the gods, I have no idea. I just...I was chasing after Meret and got caught in an earthquake, or a landslide or something, but there was something that felt very wrong about it..." He tried to puzzle out his thoughts, but no clear picture came into focus. Fuck.

"Anyways." Tjety glanced at their makeshift camp. Most of the villagers who were mobile were focused on one task or another. "How are you and the others holding up?"

Ruia shrugged and then sat down in front of him. "Well enough, I guess. Most of them didn't get much sleep." She rubbed her red-rimmed eyes. "I didn't either, for that matter."

"I don't think any of us did. It was a damned hard night." The fight against Meret and his bandits and those strange unliving creatures had been brutal. They'd managed to win the night but at the cost of another four dead villagers and more wounded survivors.

Tjety gestured toward the Iteru, Kekhmet's largest river, flowing nearby. "Did we get the last of the bodies into the river? I think I passed out at some point."

"You did, but we managed well enough. We did like you suggested—stripped the bandits and tossed them into the river. We took more time with our people, and…" Ruia drifted off, but then shook her head and refocused on him with a flinty look in her eyes that both surprised and impressed him.

"And we gave our people their last rites and sent them all into Hapi's embrace. They're on the way to the Duat now. May they find peace and joy at the Lord Osiris's gentle judgment."

He echoed the prayer, then asked, "Your da was among them?"

Ruia dropped her gaze to the ground but then lifted it up again. Without tears, she nodded. "He was. And my brother Paneb. He was in that wagon as well. I'd missed seeing him earlier. Hopefully they're with my ma now." She shrugged. "I don't know what happened to my sisters. They weren't in any of the wagons."

He frowned. "I didn't find any youngsters in my search of the village after the attack. Maybe they found a place to hide."

She stared toward the river again, then turned back to him with another shrug. "I hope so. I don't know." She gave him what looked like a half-hearted smile. "Can we find them by using this *hekau* power you think I have?"

Tjety nodded. "If we were rested and closer to the village? Possibly." He sighed. "But do you think it's the right choice to go back to the village to look for your sisters?"

She stared at him but didn't seem to be looking at him. After a long moment of silence, she refocused on his face and shook her head. In a flat voice, she said, "No. We get everyone to Fort Sekhmet and then figure out where to go from there. I guess it's the responsible thing to do."

He got his feet underneath him and stood on shaky legs, pleased that he didn't have to throw his good arm out to her for support. He was tired, hungry, and weak. He needed rest and food to recharge his battered *hekau* reserves, but it was what it was. He'd have to make do.

"I know it's a hard choice to make, Ruia. Sometimes we have to do what's responsible even when it's not what we want."

She stood as well. "I know that. One of the things you pick up as you become an adult, I guess."

He glanced at her and grunted an assent. She still wore the sidelock of youth, but she was rapidly turning into and sounding like any other adult he'd known. The shit she'd gone through the last few days must have aged her prematurely. He shook his head. So much for a gentle coming of age.

Tjety stared toward the west. Somewhere out there was the person responsible for sending the bandits and those creatures after her village. He was going to find that fucker and balance the scales. It could have been his village, his people.

He pulled his thoughts back to the present. He and the villagers had managed to kill ten bandits and about a dozen of those unliving creatures. He glanced at Ruia. "Did any of your people turn up the body of that scarred man, Qebsenuf?"

She led him toward one of the fires, around which most of the villagers were eating a modest breakfast that stank like warmed-over slop. Tjety's nose wrinkled in distaste even as his empty stomach lurched with longing.

Ruia said, "No, a few of us spiraled out from the camp and checked the trees, the old trader's road, and walked up and down the river coast a couple hundred steps in both directions. No other bodies. There are at least a couple horses missing from the picket line, aside from the ones that are dead."

Tjety nodded to some of the villagers as he found a seat among them. One of the men handed him a dented plate of food and a dirty spoon. Without thinking too hard about what exactly was on the plate, he sniffed the food then shoveled it into his mouth. It tasted awful, but it was hot and felt damn good going down.

Tjety glanced at Ruia, who was also working her way through a plate of food. "So I guess Qebsenuf got away." He glanced at the other villagers, who looked at him with a mix of curiosity and weariness. "Which means he'll be riding hard back to this quarry of theirs and reporting in to his master." He pointed toward the trader's road. "And then I suspect he and his allies are going to be coming back here with a vengeance."

Ruia stared at him, the worry evident in her eyes. "Can we get out of here before they return?"

He met her eyes, and held her look for a long moment as he considered the variables. "Damned if I know, Ruia. If your people do as I ask and keep moving, I think we can make it to Fort Sekhmet. If not, then we may well get ambushed during the day or sometime tonight."

He glanced around the fire at the various villagers. "If that happens, I don't think we'll all make it to the fort alive." He paused, took a deep breath. "We may lose more folks before we get there."

Ruia met his eyes. He saw something hard slide down over her face, some degree of toughness that he saw every time he looked into the river.

The eyes of a gods-damned survivor.

Ruia said, "The old and the weak will die. The rest of us will make it."

Some of the villagers gasped or muttered quietly amongst themselves. Tjety quirked a smile. "We'll do what we can to make sure as many of us as possible make it to the fort. We don't leave anyone behind if we can do anything about it. We're not them." He gestured toward the flowing river and where the bandits had been tossed.

Ruia licked off her spoon and dropped it and the plate onto the ground. "I've already had people gather what supplies and weapons we could find. And we fed and watered the horses." She offered him a brief smile. "Your Heker is doing all right. I think he'd like to see you."

Tjety's spirits perked up at that. He dropped his spoon and plate onto hers with a clatter and wiped his hands on his dirty tunic. "Much obliged, Ruia. Thank you for tending to him." He stood up and cleared his throat, spat aside the sludge he'd produced.

He gave the group a glance and said, "I know the last few days have been hard going. I ain't gonna lie—today and probably tomorrow will be worse.

Stick together as you have, and follow me and Ruia. We'll get you to the fort."

Some of the villagers nodded, but he saw a lot of speculative looks and outright fear writ large on most of their faces. And he fucking couldn't blame them. He shrugged his wounded arm, wincing anew at the pain. What kind of confidence could they have in a wounded Ranger just as bloodied up as they were?

Tjety focused on each of them in turn. "I have no inspiring words for you. Just honesty and truth. I think you deserve that much. The men that attacked your village were cultists of some sort, possibly a new cult of Apep."

Some of the villagers made warding signs while others gasped in surprise or shook their heads in fear.

"I checked the bandits I killed in the village and a couple we killed last night. They were each missing an ear and had similar snake-head tattoos. I'm guessing they're all cultists, but it's clear they're not a disciplined bunch."

He shifted the sling on his shoulder. "I'll be fuckin' honest with you all—if I were here alone, I'd grab a rifle and my horse and go riding after this Qebsenuf and shoot him down before he reached that quarry. But, when I was in your village, among your people… I laid the seven of them to rest in your communal hall and I made a promise."

Tjety glanced at Ruia. "I promised them I'd see you all safely to Fort Sekhmet and that I'd balance the scales so that whoever was responsible for the attack on your home, for the hurts you've suffered, would pay for what they'd done."

He rested his good hand on the pommel of his pistol. "And as a Ranger of Mayat, I make that promise to you as well."

The villagers glanced at each other, some palming away tears while others just stared, tired or sullen or wounded. None seemed interested in speaking up. He was afraid most of their spirits had been squashed.

Ruia moved to stand next to him and addressed the others. "Tjety's done a lot for us, and we've all worked together. Let's pack up and get moving. We've got a long day ahead of us."

She turned away from them and reached out to squeeze his good arm. "Thanks for your words, Tjety. They mean a lot, even if none of them say so."

He glanced down at her and patted her shoulder. "Thanks. I'll check out the weapons and the horses. Get the supplies and your wounded loaded up into the best wagon."

She brushed her hands off on her shift dress. "Already started. But thanks. We'll get rolling soon enough."

Tjety rested a hand on her shoulder and smiled what he hoped was an encouraging smile, then moved over to the now-empty buckboard wagon, where the villagers had stacked up the weapons and ammunition they had scrounged from the bandits.

There were six pistols and four lever-action rifles, fairly old by modern standards but entirely functional. There were enough rounds for one reload per pistol, plus about twenty rounds left over that he placed into a small canvas bag. The rifles were fortunately of the same caliber and there were enough rounds for each rifle to have three rounds. His own pistol was fully reloaded from the supply out his satchel that had somehow stayed strapped to Heker's back all through the encounters over the last couple of days. But beyond that he had just seven more rounds, and none of the other pistols in the wagon were of the same make or caliber as his. Once he'd shot these thirteen rounds, he'd have to resort to another pistol or rifle, or hope that he could get into blade range and make use of his khopesh.

Tjety then turned his attention to the string of

horses, smiling in spite of his weariness at Heker's perked-up ears and snorts of welcome as he approached. He ran his hands along Heker's neck and rested his forehead against his mount's head. "Damn good to see you, buddy. I hope you got more sleep than I did."

Heker snorted, then nudged Tjety's chest with his nose. Tjety scratched at a spot between his ears and enjoyed a few precious seconds getting lost in his long friendship with Heker.

Tjety offered a prayer to Amun-Re for the good fortune surrounding Heker, then stroked Heker's flank. "I don't know how you managed to survive everything that's happened over the last couple days, but I'm damned grateful all the same."

Heker wobbled his head and nearly knocked him over with another nose-butt to the chest, but Tjety maintained his feet. He patted Heker's nose, and then pulled away so that he could focus on the other horses. The sun was rising in the sky and they were losing valuable time. A tickle in his *hekau* suggested that they had to get moving soon. It was going to be a damned hard day.

A STREAM OF ANCIENT Kekhmetic hieroglyphs floated through Zezago's mind's eye, connecting and disconnecting in patterns and then rushing past in random fashion. The steady flow of glyphs and strange meanings burned off the lingering weariness he felt and then faded from view. He pushed himself to full wakefulness. He had indulged in a slow morning, recharging his *hekau* after a long night monitoring that Ranger and the survivors of the little battle that had taken place during the night.

His thin lips settled into a scowl. He opened his eyes and glanced around the interior of his large canvas tent, and focused on his silent construct standing to one side of the closed door flaps. The mummified form, its glowing green eyes and heart scarab pulsing softly in the shadows within the tent, stood with a carafe of wine in its hands and Zezago's chain of servant's ears draped around its neck. The moldy wrappings encasing its body were tattered and hung off it in fragments, and the thing had a dank, earthy smell that wasn't entirely unpleasant.

Zezago focused on the chain of trophies, reminded of the soldiers who had pledged their service and their lives to him. Many now lay dead because of that Ranger and his newfound allies. "Explain to me how an upstart Ranger and a slip of a girl manage to stage a counter-attack and win their freedom against my soldiers and your kin?"

The construct simply stared at him, though he fancied he could guess what it was thinking. "Indeed. Where there is a will, there is a way. Their will to survive was stronger than my men's collective will to complete their task. Unfortunate."

Zezago pushed himself up to a sitting position, stifling a cough as he waved the construct over. He took the carafe of wine and downed a couple mouthfuls of the water-weakened vintage, smothering the next few coughs that threatened to spasm his chest. He handed the carafe back to the construct.

"Clearly we need to obtain more dedicated soldiers, or I need to work harder at instilling stronger discipline in the ones I have." He glanced at the construct sharply, imagining a faint rebuke.

"Oh, no, I don't blame your kin for the failure. They were ineffectively built. It's not their fault I have inferior materials upon which to work my *hekau*. Had I something better to work with than this quarry's soft limestone, the spells and incantations might set better, but…" Zezago waved the next comment aside. "No matter. We'll continue to scout or trade for better quality stone. Hush now, and let me think."

The construct took a few steps back to stand by the closed tent flaps. Zezago rested his sandaled feet on the ground. The only survivor of his from the battle was his overseer, Qebsenuf, who was already on his way back to the quarry camp. He'd seen the man sneak away from the fight leading a horse. He'd be back in the camp later in the day, most likely, but Zezago didn't have time to wait for his return.

He glanced at his construct again. "I'm tempted to discipline Qebsenuf again, but no. He is too valuable to waste." He mused on the matter at hand, and then nodded. "I'll need his help in the field, and beyond that, his services will be required more than ever here to get the slaves working hard again."

Zezago stood up and stretched, then reached for his knee-length kilt and strapped it around his waist. "Now, that Ranger. I'm confident he'll want to lead the survivors to Fort Sekhmet. It's the only refuge anywhere close, and he's both wounded and shepherding wounded villagers."

He glanced at the construct. "Of course not. They're wounded and have few horses. They'll be forced to move slowly. Easy targets."

Zezago slipped on his dark robes and then wrapped his headcloth around his head and neck. He pulled his sword and scabbard off the tent pole, and then moved toward the tent flaps. The construct pushed one of them aside, spilling sunlight into the tent.

Zezago nodded. "See to cleaning up the tent and then prepare my things for a hard ride today." Without waiting for an answer, he left his tent and headed toward the edge of his camp, enjoying the early warmth of the morning sunrise on his face as he took in the measure of his operation.

His slaves and constructs were already clanging away with hammers and chisels at the old quarry's dull gray limestone walls. Some of the workers piled the seemingly-endless stream of fist-sized limestone rocks into wagons. Other constructs wheeled those wagons to a larger tent at the outskirts of the camp, on a rocky rise overlooking the camp. There, he would conduct rituals to turn those rocks into more heart amulets for use in bringing new life to the bodies and mummies his men were bringing to the camp.

The camp itself was set into a narrow valley surrounded by limestone cliffs, and soldiers with rifles and keen eyes were stationed at regular intervals around the cliff edges. There weren't as many cooking fires burning in front of his men's tents, and he was again reminded of the losses he had suffered.

Smoke from the cook's fires suggested that the morning meal was underway. He signaled one of his soldiers over from where he ate with some friends. "Your boss is returning to the camp, but while he is away, I'm making you the camp chief."

The soldier blinked at him, gaping around a mouthful of eggs and bacon. Before the man had a chance to embarrass himself further, Zezago added, "Your task is to assemble thirty fighting men, an equal number of constructs, and get them all ready to ride out. Can you handle that?"

The soldier nodded, swallowed noisily, and then opened his mouth to speak. Zezago cut him off with a curt nod and a wave of his hand. "Then get on with it."

As the man scampered off in the direction of the limestone quarry, Zezago strapped his sword belt around his waist and settled it more comfortably on his hip. He strode over to the cook's tent, near a pair of large cooking fires and a goodly but dwindling supply of barrels, crates, and sacks of provisions. It took a few minutes for the cook to notice his presence, but once he did, he rushed over and bowed deeply.

Zezago smiled and nodded at the man. "The aromas in the air tell me you have something special planned for the morning meal, Knefa."

Knefa lifted his head and furrowed his brow. "It's little more than camp bread and a few goose eggs the scouts were able to forage, Master Deshi. And the last slabs of salted bacon. But, you flatter me."

Zezago smiled. "I value your efforts, even out here in this awful wilderness. Would that were were back home among comfortable walls and more plentiful provisions, eh?"

Knefa lowered his eyes in deference. "I hope I am not overstepping my place when I say that I hope our time away from the comforts of home is brief."

Zezago's smile faltered, but he rallied and grinned. "A good hope." He turned serious. "After the morning meal is served and completed, prepare trail rations for myself and thirty men. We'll be riding out shortly."

Knefa stared at him, then nodded. "Will you need me to accompany you?"

Zezago fished around in one of the supply barrels arranged around Knefa's tent and pulled out a spotty pear. "That won't be necessary. I need you here to continue feeding the workers and the guards left here at camp. The rest of us will be out in the field campaigning. I expect we'll be gone a couple days, three at the most."

"I'll see that it's done, Master Deshi."

Zezago saluted him with the pear before turning and heading back toward his tent. He'd get ready for battle and then join his soldiers and ride out to meet Qebsenuf. Then, they'd all intercept and capture that Ranger and the others. When Zezago brought them all back here, he would delight in breaking their spirit.

He glanced up at the rising sun and the cloudless blue sky, and smiled as he took a bite out of the pear. It would be a fine day for a hunt.

RUIA WORKED WITH HER fellow villagers to gather supplies and load them into the better of the two covered wagons. Once the supplies were loaded, she started helping the children and the wounded into the wagon as well.

One of the villagers, Sefer, glanced at her as he helped little Nauny up into the wagon. "Do you think we can trust this Ranger, Ruia?"

"I'd say we do, Sefer. Even wounded, he's a better fighter than any of us. If we have any hope of reaching the fort, we'll be better off with him than not." She glanced at the other villagers, who had turned curious eyes on her. "I, for one, trust the Ranger. I think you should, too."

Sefer nodded, apparently satisfied, and then turned back to his work. Another villager, a regular troublemaker named Setesk, rolled a barrel over to the wagon and pushed it over onto one of its ends. "You sure going to the fort is a good idea, Ruia? I think we'd just be better off heading home."

A couple of the villagers muttered agreement. One of the little boys started to wail. Ruia shook her head and then lifted her hands high, remembering how the justified dead Elder Intef did so time and again to get everyone's attention in the village hall. "Please. We don't have time to argue."

Setesk scratched at the stubble on his chin with a grimy hand. "But the village is our home. We should rebuild. Show them bandits that while they can kill some of us, they can't break our spirit."

The villagers listening in muttered, sounding like they agreed with Setesk. Ruia raised her voice to be heard over all of them. "There's nothing to stop the bandits from coming after us again. And we'll be fewer than before, and they'll just keep coming until we are all killed, turned into slaves, or..." she paused, horrified at the thought that leapt to her mind. "Or be turned into one of their unliving creatures."

Surprised looks, sobs, and muttered prayers answered her. Ma Pemra raised her hand. "How far is the fort from here?"

Ruia said, "The Ranger said it's at least fourteen hours from here. But that's one horse and one rider."

"One horse and rider, moving fast." She turned to see Tjety move up to join her and the others at the wagon.

He continued, "We have six horses, including my own. Two of them will be pulling this wagon. There's no way we'll make that kind of time with a wagon and wounded. We'll push to make the best time we can, but I expect we'll have to make camp tonight somewhere on the other side of the river and then reach the fort sometime tomorrow."

Tjety glanced at her and nodded. She blinked, the enormity of the task before them fully sinking in.

Ruia sighed. "So. A very long, hard day and night and another day ahead of us. We have some food, but we'll have to forage on the way."

One of the younger boys, Henturu, piped up. "We could fish in the river along the way!"

Ruia nodded. "If we can take some of the spare rope, we may be able to fashion some fishing nets. Good thought, Henturu." She glanced at a pair of older mas from the village, twin crones, Gheti and Matti. "Do you two feel up to knotting a couple of fishing nets?"

The older of the two sisters, Gheti, nodded. "Whatever it takes, my dear."

Ruia nodded, then raised her hands again. "Then let's get moving. Gather what you can easily carry. We leave as soon as possible."

She backed off from them and turned to join Tjety. The villagers sat as a group for a few moments, stunned and weary, but then in ones and twos moved to finish the last of their tasks.

Tjety said, "You and the others fought hard. You should be proud."

She looked askance at him. "I don't think it's fair of me to feel proud when so many of us have been lost." She waved at the empty uncovered cart, the one that had so recently been full of her dead friends and da and brother. She looked away before tears could spring to her eyes again. "I sure hope we're making the right call."

Tjety reached over and lifted her chin up with a gentle, calloused hand. "We're making the only choice that makes any fuckin' sense. We can't go back to your village and the only place we're going to find a healer for the wounded anywhere around here is Fort Sekhmet. The governor's palace in Port Raferdam is at least two weeks' ride. Too damn far."

He then glanced west, toward the low foothills leading to the mountains. "Out there somewhere is our enemy. We depleted his numbers, but I'm sure he has more to spare." Tjety slapped his good hand against his thigh, just above his leather greaves. "And I bet Qebsenuf is going to tell his boss how few we are, and they'll send enough to overwhelm us."

She frowned. "What can we do to slow them down?"

Tjety scratched at his stubble. "First thing is to get your people on their way toward the fort. Have some of them catch fish if they can do it quick and if you think it'll give them something to do other than walk and pray." He looked pensive, then added, "You should stay with the wagon. Do your best to keep everyone together and don't let anyone wander off alone, not even to relieve themselves in the woods."

"Why?" she asked.

He pointed toward the woods and hefted a broken heart amulet in his hand. "We have no idea if any of those unliving things are still out there. We killed… destroyed…several of them last night, but I don't know how many there were to begin with. Do you?"

She thought about it but shook her head. "I didn't spend much time looking at them, much less counting them."

He nodded and stowed the broken amulet in his satchel along with a couple others. "We pair everyone up. Two stand a better chance of fighting one of those things than one. They're not very smart and they're not very fast, but they're tough and stronger than they look. Beat them, knock them down, and break them apart."

She replayed his words and then frowned. "Where are you going to be? You said you wanted me with the caravan..."

"I'm going to be lagging behind. I want to make sure we're not followed. But, if we are, I will do what I can to discourage the enemy from approaching too quickly." He flexed his wounded arm, winced, and then added, "Maybe I'll ask a couple of your villagers to come with me. I don't think I can do much alone."

He raised a hand when she took a breath to protest. "I won't be far behind. Heker may look chunky, but he can eat up a lot of ground quick. He has a little bit of a runner in him."

She followed his gaze to his horse. She turned back to him, hating the petulant feeling welling up in her. "Are you sure you have to ride behind? I bet I'm not the only one who would feel safer knowing you're with us."

He shook his head. "I *will* be with you, Ruia. But I need to slow down our enemy. I think it's the only way we'll make it to the fort with any hopes of getting there with most of your—our people together."

She stared at him for a long moment, then slowly nodded. "All right, then." She nudged her chin toward his sling. "And what of you? That wound does not look good, Tjety."

He flexed it and covered it with his hand protectively. "It's damn sore but I think I'll be all right. I burned out the worst of it last night." He shrugged and then smiled, but she didn't see any truth in his eyes.

He added, "I'll take a minute before we leave and change the bandage. This one is filthy."

And it was. She wrinkled her nose at it, hoping the smell was coming from the dirt and grime, and not the wound itself. She had seen a deep cut fester on one of her friends, and it had been an ugly sight. Her friend had been left with a scar, though now she was dead, so it probably didn't matter anyway.

"All right. I'm not happy about it, but we'll do it your way, Tjety."

He stood up and offered his hand to her. "Thanks, Ruia. I wouldn't be here now if it wasn't for you. I'm grateful."

She felt the tears welling up in her eyes again, and he must have sensed it because he held her hand a little longer, and then gently pulled her to him and hugged her. She was crushed against his leathers and linens, and she could smell his wound and sweat and the blood that had dried on him.

A strange calmness washed over her, and she felt a flutter deep in her stomach from what he'd called her *hekau*. She frowned, realizing somehow that the sensation wasn't of her making. She glanced up at him. "What...what was that?"

"That was a little flexing of my *hekau* to help give you strength. I hope you don't mind."

She took a half-step away from him, trying to ferret out her feelings. The sadness that had been about to overwhelm her had lessened. She could still feel the grief, like a dam waiting to burst, but instead of one that felt like it was about to overflow and break through at any moment, it now felt like it had been strengthened by something, maybe faith and willpower of some sort that wasn't entirely hers, but not entirely unwelcome either. She reached up for the amulet around her neck and held it tight. It pulsed in time with her heartbeat and her reinvigorated *hekau*.

"Thank you. I feel...better?" She shrugged, then raised her free hand. "But...I want you to ask me before doing something like that again."

"I'm sorry, Ruia. I didn't mean to impose. I'll ask first in the future." He tried a smile. "I have plenty to learn too."

She nodded but didn't return the smile. "We should get moving."

"Right."

She led the way back to the wagon. Tjety moved over to a small group of villagers and started asking around for volunteers. In short order, two men, Mut and Khepri, and a woman, Yufa, offered to help. Tjety led them to the wagon with the weapons and helped them load up with pistols and rifles. He sent them over to the horses and then returned to Ruia.

"Take the rest of the weapons out of the wagon and spread them around to whoever can use one. Save enough shots to fire three times into the air if you run into serious problems. I'll try and keep an ear open for you and I'll come riding as hard and as fast as I can."

Ruia pulled herself up into the wagon with the rest of her people and glanced at Aniba, the village's best horse driver, who had hitched two horses to the wagon.

Aniba settled onto the seat and nodded to her. "Whenever you're ready, Ruia."

She turned to Tjety. He stepped back and raised a hand. "Get moving, Ruia. Remember that no matter what you hear, don't stop for anything. Get these people across the bridge and then to the fort."

She nodded. "Good luck, Tjety. May the gods ride with you." She felt a twinge from her amulet and fancied she caught a glimmer of the Lady Mayat in the depths of her mind's eye.

He nodded, and said, "May they ride with us all." He stepped away from the wagon and raised a hand to her in farewell.

Ruia matched the gesture and then stepped past her friends in the wagon and pulled herself up to the seat next to Aniba. "Let's move."

She forced herself to look forward as Aniba guided the horses and wagons to the old trader's road and headed south, the villagers able to walk falling into place around the wagon. But her thoughts were with Tjety and the villagers they'd left behind.

ZEZAGO RODE AT THE head of his column, thirty armed men on horseback and thirty constructs strong. He hated taking labor off the quarry, but didn't have much choice. The living slaves were too likely to try and escape, while the constructs would follow orders without question.

Zezago followed the old path down the quarry line to the dried-out causeway that once connected the quarry to the Iteru, and then followed that along a wide curve to the southeast until the causeway ran into the trader's road. He knew the road eventually ended up at Kekhmet's capital far to the south, though he had not yet ventured so far. Someday he'd get there, with a mighty column of unstoppable immortal soldiers at his back, but that day was yet some time in the future. There was much to do to get to that point, and the current issues he had to deal with were hampering his progress at every step.

He rode in silence, feeling the sun warm his face and his body through his dark robes and headcloth. It looked like it would be a bright and clear day, a good day for chasing down slaves and pressing them into his service.

After a brief rest for a high noon meal along the side of the road, he encouraged his men back into the saddle and pushed them onward. As they rode, a lone rider coming north made him pause, and then he brought the column to a halt as the rider approached. He smiled darkly as he recognized his lieutenant.

As he rode up, Qebsenuf covered a confused look with a bow from the saddle of his weary-looking horse. "Master Deshi." He brought his head up and stared at the array of troops and constructs.

Zezago said, "Our meeting is well-timed, Qebsenuf. I see you are short a number of slaves and all of my men."

Qebsenuf shifted in his saddle. "My apologies, Master Deshi. I present myself to you for punishment. I was unable to secure Meret and his charges. He and his companions lingered at the village for too long and were beset by a Ranger of Mayat. This same Ranger we took captive and beat severely, but he was able to rally the survivors and gain their freedom."

Zezago smiled, patient. Qebsenuf couldn't possibly know that he had observed the end of the battle from the air. "And your men?"

Qebsenuf shook his head. "Dead on the field. I managed to escape before I met their fate." Qebsenuf added, "I am sorry, Master Deshi. I have failed you."

Zezago raised a hand. "You *did* fail, Qebsenuf, but you are not solely responsible for this debacle. I place blame at the feet of Meret as well." He paused, considered the circumstances. "A Ranger of Mayat, you say? Tell me more as we ride." He heeled his horse forward, signaling to the troops to follow.

Qebsenuf wheeled his horse around and rode alongside him. "His headcloth and weapons marked him clearly as a Ranger. He had shot Meret and was about to finish him off when we rode up and confronted him. I had hoped Meret would survive, but last night when we made camp before pushing on to the quarry, the Ranger and the survivors staged a revolt and overpowered Meret and the rest of my men."

"And the villagers? How did they manage to marshal the strength and will to fight?"

Qebsenuf shrugged. "I suppose the desire to be free gave them the strength they needed."

Zezago nodded. "As any strong-willed person might have done."

Qebsenuf glanced at the armed men riding behind them. "The villagers are hurt and tired, Master Deshi. If we push hard, we should be able to catch up to them before they reach the crossroads and the bridge."

"Where do you think they'll go, once they reach the crossroads?" Zezago stared closely at his lieutenant, hoping there was some glimmer of intelligence within that scarred visage.

Qebsenuf considered it and then glanced at him. "I suppose the smartest route for them would be to make for the Kekhmet fort some hours ride from the river. I don't see another option that makes any sense."

Zezago nodded approvingly. "Well reasoned, Qebsenuf. That is my assessment as well. Now, next question. Given the variables you see before you and the resources stretched out behind us, what would your next step be?"

Qebsenuf again glanced at the soldiers and constructs marching along behind, and then turned to face the path ahead. His face furrowed in concentration. "There's just one bridge across the river anywhere nearby and that's at the crossroads. The Ranger and the villagers will reach that bridge before we do. There's simply no time for us to get around them that way."

Zezago nodded, but remained silent. The test wasn't a hard one, but could his man work it through?

Qebsenuf continued. "There are two fords across the river in this province; one a short ride to the north, and a second farther south from the bridge. The last one is too far to be of use for us, but the northern one..."

Zezago glanced at him and offered a gentle prod. "Yes?"

Qebsenuf looked to be hard in thought, then nodded slowly. "We could split our column up into two companies, send one northeast through the ford and then south, while the other column moves south and then east over the bridge."

"A pincers movement?"

Qebsenuf nodded. "Something like that. The column fording the river would be slowed, but I seem to recall the terrain on the other side of the river is pretty clear." He looked vaguely in the direction of the ford, and nodded. "If we timed it right, we could get ahead of the Ranger and his caravan and catch them in a vise."

Zezago pulled up reins, and Qebsenuf and the column behind him stopped. Zezago beamed at Qebsenuf. "You've worked through the problem, my good man. Well done. How would you feel about leading that second column across the river?"

Qebsenuf raised an eyebrow. "If you feel confident entrusting me with such a task, then I would be honored to do so."

Zezago waved off the man's comments. "You are an able lieutenant, Qebsenuf. One setback is not enough for me to purge you from my service." He lowered his voice and leaned in so that only Qebsenuf could hear. "And besides, you are the only one I trust. I have no one else as reliable as you."

Zezago settled back in his saddle and waved Qebsenuf toward the column of troops. "Go. Take all of the constructs and half the men. Ride hard to the ford, cross the river, and then make best speed to the fort."

Qebsenuf grinned, unable to conceal his delight. How foolishly trusting he was.

Zezago fished around in his satchel for an amulet

and after some rummaging, found the one he was looking for. It was a dense chunk of obsidian, roughly filed down and shaped into an arrowhead. One side had been worked to a smooth surface on which was etched finely-detailed letters in his native tongue. It pulsed softly in his hands with the latent power he had laced into it.

He closed his eyes and reached into the thing with his *hekau* to trigger the power there. The arrowhead pulsed once in his hands, then he tossed it to Qebsenuf, who caught it neatly out of the air. Qebsenuf stared at it with curiosity.

Zezago answered his unspoken question. "It's a simple signaling device, little more than a magical sparker. When you and your column are in position on the road, loose it into the air as high as you can. It will explode and signal to me that you are ready. I will keep a watchful eye out for it."

Qebsenuf shoved the amulet into his satchel. "I'll do as you command, Master Deshi. Thank you for your faith in me."

Zezago waved him toward the troops. "Go now, Qebsenuf. Do not fail me again."

His lieutenant heeled his horse down the line of troops, shouting out orders to them. He paused near the line of constructs and uttered a few brief commands, and then without another glance, led his column through the trees, heading for the river shore.

Zezago watched them leave, then raised a hand to the remainder of his troops. "Come, we have prey to catch."

AS A LIGHT BREEZE rippled through the trees lining the river shore, Tjety held Heker's reins and watched the caravan move down the road. He raised his hand in farewell. A couple of the wounded adults in the back of the wagon and one child raised their hands in response. He sighed, hoping he wasn't making a huge mistake sending them on ahead alone, but then shook his head and mounted Heker.

He settled onto Heker's back and wheeled him around to face the northern end of the old trader's road. The three villagers who had volunteered to ride with him, Khepri, Mut, and Yufa, were already mounted and waiting.

He put heel to Heker and walked over. "The deaths of your friends are an affront to Mayat and all she stands for and all that I have pledged to enforce. Their deaths demand justice be served." He gestured with his wounded arm, in a sling made of his headcloth. "I can't hope to stop the threat coming for us alone, and I am grateful for your help."

The taller man, Mut, nodded and then spat a stream of dark liquid off to the far side of his horse. He must have secured some chewing weed from one of the dead bandits. "Just tell us what we can do to help, Ranger." He touched the bandit pistol hanging from his waist. "I'm not great with a gun but I can scrap with the best of 'em."

Tjety nodded and walked Heker past them. "Just keep up as best you can and we'll figure something out on the way north. My hope is that we can set up some form of roadblock and slow down any approaching riders. I don't know what Qebsenuf has at his disposal, but we have to guess it's mounted men and more of those walking unliving things."

The three villagers fell in with him and followed him along the road. It was clear that none of them were experienced riders, though they all kept to their mounts well enough. He felt a strong sense of pride that all three of them had left the bandits' Hesso-made saddles behind, favoring bareback riding with just bridles and blankets in the traditional Kekhmetic manner. Things couldn't be all bad on the frontier if folks resisted the newer Hesso ways.

The lone woman to volunteer, Yufa, rode with knees and heels as she used both hands to work her thick black hair into a serviceable queue and then tied it off with a length of leather cord. Once finished, she took the reins with her hands and glanced at Tjety. "What are you doing this far north, Ranger? Thought your kind were all in the deep south, fighting the Kesh."

"Most of them are fighting with Pharaoh's regulars. I picked the empty cup and got posted north for my trouble." Tjety thrust his good hand vaguely southward. "I'm here on the fuckin' sufferance of Pharaoh and of my superiors at Karam Oasis." Uttering the name of the Rangers' headquarters left a foul taste in his mouth. Bastards.

The shorter and swarthier of the two men, Khepri, snorted but kept his eyes forward on the road, clutching the carbine he'd appropriated from one of the dead bandits. "Sounds like you maybe had an indiscretion or two and ended up getting posted way out here more outta spite."

Tjety shot him a glare but didn't deny the statement. He simply offered a Hesso swear he must have picked up from Meret. "Anyways. As the only fuckin' Ranger on the northern fuckin' frontier, it's up to me to find the truth about what's happening and then mete out justice to whoever's responsible." He pumped his fist toward the north. "Somewhere up ahead is that person. I can *feel* it."

And he could, even though his *hekau* was still below full strength, depleted from the actions over the last couple days. The bit of sleep he had managed to catch last night plus the little bit of food he'd eaten before they broke camp had helped, though. He also had several waterskins draped on Heker's back, and he wasn't shy about drinking them dry. Water might not taste as good as beer, but there was no denying the healing benefits of drinking it frequently.

He settled his gear and newly-acquired rifle on the satchels in front of and behind him, and moved Heker forward into a trot. The three villagers likewise put heel to their horses to keep pace.

Tjety led them north, scanning either side of the road as they rode, looking for something specific. After a solid hour of steady riding, he found what he'd been looking for, or at least something damned close. He slid off Heker's back and secured the horse's reins to a stout tree, then pulled the axe he'd appropriated from the dead bandits out of his collection of supplies. The villagers pulled up rein around him. Tjety glanced at Mut and handed the axe to him.

Tjety gestured to the trees along both sides of the road. "This is the densest area of trees I've seen up to now, and if we can chop a few of them down, we should be able to block this road. The undergrowth is too dense here to allow a horse and rider passage."

Mut nodded and took the axe, and without hesitation scanned the treeline along the road and picked a likely candidate. He swung the axe and the sharp blade bit into the trunk. Khepri glanced at Tjety and shrugged, then produced a second hand axe and joined his companion.

Yufa stayed on her horse and glanced toward the river. "What about the shore? If riders *can* find a way through the trees, they could get past the blockade by following the river."

Tjety walked toward the river through a break in the trees. "That's why I was thinking we could also drop a few trees along the coastline. Block up both the road and the coastline, maybe force the riders to take the river ford way up north."

Yufa shook her head. "I didn't know there was another ford other than the one near our village."

Tjety waved at her to follow, the grunts of the two men and their axes hitting trees sounding in the background. "One of the maps Pharaoh's scouts had prepared before I left the Asyut garrison showed a northern ford. It's too far for us to use, but if we can choke up these two areas, we can force our enemy to use it."

He swung his axe one-handed through some of the undergrowth to clear a path to the shoreline, then jogged north along the shore until he found a spot where the river ran nearly up against the trees. He checked the shore and the river, and was encouraged to see a nice bonus—here the flow of the river had worn down the shore line enough so that there was a relatively steep drop from the coast into the river. He glanced at Yufa. "This is perfect. They'll have a hard time getting around this unless they want to fuckin' swim."

He hefted the axe in his good hand and awkwardly started cutting into the trees abutting the river. After a moment, Yufa fell in next to him and hacked away at the smaller branches with a long knife. Tjety focused on the medium-sized trees, striking a balance between knowing they didn't have time to cut down the big ones and that the little trees wouldn't serve as enough of an obstacle.

After laying in some hard work, he had what he wanted, or at least close enough to get the job done. Four medium-width trees fallen, largely blocking the space between the dense tree line and the river. If anyone were to chase after them and want to use the shore as passage, they'd get stopped here and would have to either go north to the ford, which would take hours, or clear the obstruction, which would also take time. Either way, he hoped that it'd be enough to buy Ruia and the other villagers the time they needed to get to the gods-damned fort.

He drained a waterskin and then nodded toward Yufa. "Now back to the road." He leaned over and refilled his waterskin in the Iteru, then hurried back to the road. Heker and Yufa's horse had wandered over to the far side of the road, and were working their way through some of the lush grass growing there. Tjety clucked at his horse but didn't pull him away from the feast.

Mut and Khepri had managed to fell a handful of large trees, and were taking a break, sweating hard and passing a waterskin back and forth. Tjety led Yufa up to them and nodded his appreciation. "Damn fine work, you two, but it's not nearly enough. We need to keep at it." He glanced up at the sun. "It's past noon. If I remember the maps right, anyone coming from the old quarry should be getting close if they're riding with a purpose."

The two men traded a look and then got back to swinging their axes. Tjety traded a look with Yufa and then joined in. It was hard going. Not only was his axe blade now duller than he would have liked, with poor bite into the trees, but it was a struggle swinging an axe with one good arm and an infection burning inside his body.

Felling the trees near the river with Yufa had worn him down, but now he was edging toward exhausted. He took more breaks to catch his breath than he would have liked, and after helping to drop a third medium-sized tree into the road, he had to call it enough and handed his axe over to Yufa.

He drained another waterskin and then directed the three villagers to use their horses to drag and stack the fallen trees into the road. It wasn't as dense a blockade as he would have liked, but it would have to do. Just looking at it made him think he'd need precious time to clear it.

Tjety said, "All right. That's enough. It'll have to do. Refill your waterskins and then let's ride like demons."

The three villagers stowed their axes and then hurried to the river. As they went, Tjety mounted Heker and then kept an eye on the horses, while also keeping an eye on the northern road beyond their roadblock. He paused and strained his senses. He'd been sure he had heard something in the distance, coming down the road. Nothing distinct struck him other than a vague hiccup in his *hekau*. He glanced at the blockade. It had to be good enough.

The wound in his arm was now a constant ache, and he flexed it briefly then winced in fresh pain. Shit. His arm wasn't getting any better and now he was starting to really feel the drain of the last couple of days. What he'd give for a few long quiet nights in a real bed next to a real fire.

He indulged in a minute or two of self-pity, then set his mouth and his will. He was not about to roll over and die in this road. He wasn't going to give anyone the satisfaction, not even the gods.

He glanced up into the sky to gauge the time, and saw a dozen or more black vultures circling high over head. They had to be checking the ground to see if there were any leavings to enjoy. Maybe they'd find something worthwhile farther down the river, perhaps a bandit's body that had washed up onto the shore or got hung up in a tangle of reeds.

Staring at the birds sparked an idea, though it was risky given his dwindling *hekau* reserves. He'd been given instruction on how to project his *ba* into the body and mind of a simple animal, and while he wasn't very good at it, mostly because he'd never given himself the time to practice, he knew the basics.

He raised his voice. "Come on, let's get moving!" In short order, the three villagers returned with dripping waterskins, and mounted their respective horses. He faced the three of them. "Yufa, Mut. Ride on. Ride as hard as you can and catch up with the wagon and the rest of your people."

All three of them frowned. Yufa was the first to speak up. "What are you and Khepri going to do?"

Tjety pointed out the vultures flying high overhead. "I have an idea, probably a damned stupid one, but I'm gonna need Khepri's help if I'm going to do it. But I don't need to keep you two in danger any more than necessary. Go on, ride." He gestured toward the road. "But ride with my thanks. I couldn't have done this work without your help."

They traded looks with each other and with Khepri, then turned to the south. Mut glanced at Tjety and nodded. "Don't be too far behind. We could use you if we do get attacked."

"We'll ride on as soon as we can."

Mut and Yufa heeled their horses and tore off down the road. Tjety glanced at Khepri. "Follow me."

Tjety walked Heker down the road and tied the reins off to a nearby tree. "Just keep an eye out for any bandits or creatures. It's going to look like I fall asleep, but I'm actually trying to do some scouting, using my Ranger training with my *hekau*."

Khepri shrugged. "I don't know such things." He cradled his carbine. "But I can keep watch just fine. Do what you need to do, Ranger."

Tjety nodded his thanks and then settled onto Heker's back. He closed his eyes and crossed his arms across his chest, cradling his wounded arm. He focused on his *ba*, and how it was connected to his body by a thin cord his trainer had called the heart-string, and imagined his *ba* flying out of his body yet still attached to that glowing silver thread.

Tjety felt the drain on his *hekau*. It was hard work to pull his *ba* out of his body. There was a strong sense of resistance all along the line, as if his body wanted that soul right where it belonged before it was time to give it up. He gritted his teeth and focused, and pushed harder against that insubstantial resistance. He felt something tear within his *hekau* and winced at the sensation. But, his *ba* pulled away from his body, the gossamer-like trail of his heart-string floating along behind it, like when he used to play out the thin string on one of his little brother's wind-toys.

He focused the greater portion of his consciousness and imagined his *ba* in the form of a bird, trusting in Khepri to keep watch over his body. He'd heard the stories of *ba*-travelers having their bodies damaged while they were in *ba*-form, and being permanently severed from their bodies and left to float around aimlessly forever, or those who had been unceremoniously snapped back to their bodies due to some sudden trauma they hadn't anticipated.

Tjety sent his *ba*-form soaring up into the afternoon sunlight. He focused on one of the wheeling buzzards, moving close to it and then steeling himself for the deep dive into its spiritual house to take temporary ownership of its body. He felt the strain even before he closed in. He tried to push his *ba* against the vulture's own primitive spiritual form, but even that was too much, too strong for him to push aside. He just didn't have the strength. The last few days had been brutal on his *hekau*.

He pushed his *ba*-bird away from the buzzard, and drifted in the air for a time, noting the long, thin, nearly-transparent cord attached to his *ba*-form, trailing all the way back down to his body far below. Inspiration struck him then. If he was too tired to take on a bird, perhaps he could just scan the horizon in this form for a few moments.

The drain on his *hekau* was significant, so he forced himself to take just a few minutes. He focused to the north, following the break in the trees that he knew was the road, trying to pick out any useful details. He found the spot where he and the others had felled the trees to block the road, and focused beyond that.

Tjety took a risk and drew more energy from his *hekau*, sending it up his heart-string and into his senses. He needed better eyesight than he now possessed, so he enhanced his vision and focused on the column of riders working their way along the trader's road.

He counted off sixteen riders, all but one in riding leathers and plain headcloths matching those the bandits had all worn. The one lone exception was riding at the head of the column, a man dressed in dark robes, riding tall in the saddle of a fine black horse. He had a sword scabbard fixed to one side of his waist and serious eyes peering out underneath the folds of his black headcloth. His expression was grim, and every muscle, every movement of his body as he rode oozed confidence and strength.

Tjety caught just the slightest flare of *hekau* about the man, and somehow he knew, without a doubt, that this was the man responsible not only for the strange unliving things roaming the countryside, but also the raid on the village. Tjety stared at him, and whether it was a whisper from Lady Mayat, or some other intuition deep within his *ba*, he knew this man was his enemy.

He felt a tug on his heart-string as he focused on the man in the dark robes. His time was up and his body was telling him it was time to return. He took one last look at the man at the head of the column and blanched, because it seemed that the man had stopped his horse and was standing up in his stirrups, staring up at his *ba*-form.

Without hesitation, Tjety grabbed hold of his heart-string and plunged toward his body, desperate to return before any possible mischief could be inflicted upon his *ba* or his body. That man and his troops were nearing the blockade and would be through it sooner than later. He had to get moving, *now*.

He slammed his soul back into his body and rocked on Heker's back. He grabbed both reins in his hands and steadied himself, and blinked several times to get his bearings. He glanced at Khepri, who looked surprised. "Time to go."

Khepri stared at him. "Are you all right? You look like you seen a spirit."

Tjety nodded. "I'm well enough, but you're right." He pointed to the north. "I saw the one responsible for the murder of your friends. He and his men are close to the barricade. We ride, now."

He heeled Heker into a quick trot and moved south along the road without another word. Khepri fell in behind him. Tjety pushed Heker into a gallop, opening up as much distance as he could between him and that man in the dark robes.

RUIA SHIFTED UNCOMFORTABLY on the driver's bench of the wagon, trying to maintain focus all around as they rode south along the road between the trees.

The driver, Aniba, glanced at her and offered a tired smile. "Relax, Ruia. You can't see everything at the same time."

She nodded, feeling the weariness in her bones. "I just feel like it's up to me to get everyone safely to the fort."

Aniba chucked the reins to keep the two horses moving. "You're a strong girl, Ruia. You're doing all right. I remember your ma and your da—both strong people, and good friends. You're their daughter and that's no lie."

She touched his arm in gratitude. "I appreciate that, Aniba, I really do."

She leaned back a bit to look into the back of the wagon. It was filled with the wounded, the children, and the two sister-crones, Gheti and Matti. She nodded her head toward them. "How are the fishing nets coming?" She tried to keep her tone light.

Matti looked up from her knotting work, her gnarled hands full of thin strands of rope. "It's going along, my dear. Should have the first one finished soon. Then we'll start on a second one."

The other sister, Gheti, muttered under her breath as she knotted strands together. "Don't know why we're knotting this when we could just shoot the damn fish out of the damn river."

Ruia said, "Tjety said we should conserve our ammunition. We don't know what we'll run into." She grinned half-heartedly. "Besides, there's no one in our little company who can shoot worth a damn. We're more likely to miss the river than hit any fish."

Gheti snorted as she continued her knotting. "Gimme one of them rifles and I'll shoot enough fish to last us a week."

Matti nudged her on the shoulder. "You ain't handled a gun in twenty years. You'd shoot off your own fool foot."

Gheti snorted. "Not me! I'd blast them fish out of the river." She made her hands, still knotted into the net in progress, into the shape of a finger rifle and mimicked shooting it into the river. "Ptah's tits, I bet I could even blast me a hippo, and then we'd have meat for a month. How'd that be?" She ran her tongue around her dry lips and the gaps in her teeth.

Ruia smiled, almost laughed, but then Setesk approached, all dour and gloomy. He was the town voice of doom and disaster, and she was somehow surprised he'd lived through the whole ordeal. His mouth usually got him into trouble.

Setesk walked up alongside the wagon. "Me and some of the other fellas been talkin'."

She braced for a bad conversation. "And what did you resolve?"

"We don't think going to the fort is the best thing for us. There's medicines and food and supplies back at the village." He indicated the wagon. "We don't have nothing to trade with here other than the few things we stole from them bandits."

Ruia raised a hand. "Hold. We didn't steal nothing. Those bandits took our village, our friends, and our lives from us. We earned the right to take what they no longer need. They went to a place where their guns and supplies won't help them."

He shook his head. "All the same, we think it's a poor idea to go to the fort." He reached up to grab her arm. "Ruia, we want you to take us home."

She stared down into his pleading eyes, and her heart spun between breaking anew for her people and hardening against the truth the Ranger had explained to her and that didn't seem to register with everyone in the caravan. A twinge from her *hekau* renewed her flagging spirits.

She pushed his hand away. "We can't do that, Setesk. I'm sorry."

He frowned. "But why? Because that Ranger told you not to? He's not one of us, Ruia. He's an outsider, new to the frontier. Besides, he didn't look like he was all there anyway, what with that gunshot and all."

She shook her head. "We're going to the fort, and that's that. We have wounded that probably wouldn't make it to the village. The fort and its healer-priests are the best hope we have of making it through this together."

He scrunched up his face as if he'd eaten something bitter, then stepped ahead to stand in front of the wagon. Aniba pulled back on the reins to stop the horses from trampling over him.

Ruia stood up. "Get out of the way, Setesk. Trust me to lead us to the fort."

Setesk stared her down. He appeared to be working up the courage to say something more.

Aniba leaned over from the wagon bench. "Come on, Setesk. Daylight's wasting and we got a long way to go. Bridge is still somewhere up ahead. Let's get there at least before we start arguin' with each other."

Setesk stared at Aniba and then, after a long moment, nodded. He faced Ruia. "To the bridge, then. Think it over, Ruia. Make the right choice." He moved away from the horses.

As Aniba slapped the leads and got the horses moving again, Setesk called up to Ruia. "We're tired, Ruia. Take us home."

She met his eyes and held the look as the wagon passed him, and then she sat back down on the bench and focused forward. She glanced at the river flowing through the trees beyond the road. Somewhere ahead was the bridge. She realized that this terrain wasn't all that unfamiliar to her. She'd run south along the river just the other day, and then had been ridden back north to the camp on a horse with Qebsenuf and the other bandits when they had taken her and Tjety captive.

She crossed her arms on her knees and rested her head on her arms. Setesk and his cronies from the village were usually just full of bluster, but out here, away from home, with guns and desperation, they could probably do just about anything. If things got violent, there'd be real problems. The last thing she wanted was a fight with her own people. But Setesk was loud and persistent, and he could get some of the others to follow his lead, even if it meant leading them to their deaths.

And she wasn't sure she had enough friends among the survivors to stand with her.

AFTER SEVERAL MINUTES OF hard riding, Tjety reined in Heker and paused for Khepri to catch up. Tjety took a few gulps from a waterskin and tried hard to ignore the burning sensation coming from the gunshot in his arm. He wiped the sweat from his forehead. Shit. He felt feverish. "You need to keep riding, Khepri. Don't wait for me."

Khepri wheeled his horse around and stared at him. "Can't leave you behind, Ranger. Ruia'd never forgive me."

Tjety stared off toward the north. Still no sign of that man in dark robes or his allies, but he knew that they had to be getting close. The makeshift roadblock couldn't have been that much of a deterrent.

He nodded to Khepri. "Go on, then. Lead the way."

Khepri heeled his horse and rode down the road. Tjety pushed Heker into a quick trot and rode alongside him. "I'm sure Ruia wouldn't think twice if you left me behind."

Khepri shrugged as he navigated the road. "I ain't so sure. She can get right feisty when questioned. I wouldn't wanna cross her, and now....now she seems different."

Tjety shrugged. "I don't know what to say. I didn't know her, before. I'll take your word for it."

He rode with Khepri around a bend in the road, and then opened up Heker to a gallop. Khepri and his borrowed horse kept up as best they could, though it was clear that the man wasn't an experienced rider. He was holding on more to keep from falling off than he was at trying to get any additional swiftness out of the animal.

Tjety slowed Heker enough to match Khepri's speed, digging deep to find the patience between the need to get as much distance between him and the dark man and the desire to not leave Khepri behind.

To his credit, Khepri held tighter onto the reins and seemed to find his seat. He and his horse picked up a little more speed, and he glanced at Tjety as they moved along the road. "You...should ride ahead, Ranger. I'm...I'm slowing you down."

Tjety shook his head. "I'm not leaving you behind, Khepri."

Tjety traded a look with him, seeing the fear in his eyes soften somewhat. After another several minutes of steady riding, Mut and Yufa appeared in the road ahead, standing their horses off to the side.

Confused, Tjety pulled up short and stopped Heker a couple arm's lengths from them. Khepri skidded to a stop nearby.

Mut offered a weak wave. "Sorry, Tjety. My horse pulled up lame. Rode him too damned hard."

Tjety cursed and glanced north up the road. No sign of pursuit as yet, though he knew it was coming. He turned back to Mut. "How bad is she?"

Mut squatted next to the horse and ran his hand down her back left leg, and pulled it up to show the underside of her hoof.

Tjety glanced at it from where he was seated on Heker's back. Shit. The horse's hoof was caked with blood and dirt. Mut poked at the bloody mess with a finger. The horse started and shifted sideways, but Mut managed to keep both his balance and the horse's leg in hand.

Mut called out to the horse to calm down, then pulled out his knife and started chipping away at the junk caked into the horse's hoof. He paused and glanced up at Tjety. "This is bad, Ranger. Even if I get all this cleaned out, she's not gonna want to put much weight down on it. Not enough to ride on, anyway."

Tjety shook his head. "She'll heal up in time, but we can't wait. Leave her and ride double with Khepri. It'll slow us down, but it's damned faster than standing here."

Mut grimaced but nodded, and dropped the horse's leg and pulled the bridle and blanket and supplies off of her and dumped it all into the bushes near the side of the road. He gathered up his weapons and then started toward Khepri and his horse.

Tjety felt a sudden spear of warning through his *hekau*. A chorus of hoofbeats sounded on the ground. Someone yelled a challenge. He turned to look north. The man in dark robes and four of his allies curved into view, thundering down the road toward them.

"Riders coming!" Tjety yelled, and pulled his pistol as the air around him erupted in gunfire from both sides. In moments, Mut went down hard, and one of the bandits was lifted out of his saddle by Khepri's rifle blast.

Tjety managed to score two direct hits on one of the bandits, sending him spinning out of his saddle. But then the dark-robed man plunged into the thick of things, his sword raised high. Tjety somehow managed to holster his pistol and clear his khopesh with his free hand to parry a powerful blow.

More gunfire blasted all around. It was impossible to tell in the furor who was still standing and who had fallen. Tjety's world had been reduced to two horses and the dark man and his flashing sword. Over and over the man thrust and swiped and cut at him, and it was all Tjety could do to counter his blows and keep Heker from spilling him into the dirt.

Another rifle shot boomed out, and out of the corner of his eye, Tjety saw Yufa fall off her horse and sprawl out into the dusty road. The bandit that had done for her took a wild shot at Tjety that missed but zipped close to the dark man, who shifted precariously in his saddle.

Desperate, Tjety heeled Heker into the man's black horse, reached down to grab the man's calf, and pulled as hard as he could.

Miraculously, the gambit worked. The dark man

toppled over the side of his black horse, swinging his sword ineffectually at Tjety, who wasted no time in putting heel to Heker and riding as fast as he could to the south. Tjety glanced back as he rode away, gritting his teeth at the two villagers lying prone on the road and the third, Khepri, slumped in the saddle, his horse walking aimlessly toward the tree line. Two of the bandits were sprawled out on the ground as well.

But then the dark man was getting to his feet, his two remaining allies helping him out. Tjety kicked Heker into the fastest gallop he could manage, and rode like mad, away from the disaster.

TJETY KEPT THEM GALLOPING for as long as he could, but eased off when he felt Heker heaving hard. As they slowed, Tjety checked his pistol, saw that it was empty, and then reloaded with a shaky hand. Enough. He had to give Heker some rest. It wasn't fair to the poor beast to ride him to death.

He pulled Heker up short along the side of the road. He took a deep swig of water from his water skin, then walked Heker through the thin tree line and over to the river's shore.

He opened up his weary *hekau* to scan for signs of beasts, but detected nothing large enough nearby to present a threat to him or his horse.

He let Heker walk into the water, the ripples lapping at his hooves. Heker lowered his head to the water and drank deeply, his flanks expanding and contracting at every swallow.

Tjety glanced up and down the river, then up toward the sun, the god Re shining down on him. This was as good a place as any for a last stand. He lifted a leg over Heker's neck and dismounted onto the wet river shore, and knelt down to refill his empty water skin. After replacing the cap, he closed his eyes.

"Mighty Mayat and eternal Hapi, look kindly upon your humble servant and help me survive the next few fucking minutes." He prayed harder than he had in a long time, and opened up his *ba* and his *hekau* for any sign, any hope that someone was listening. At first, nothing, but then…something, a slow trickle of energy slipping from the river and into his *hekau*. Not a lot, but even that little was a wonderment, a sign that perhaps something had changed—some understanding between him and the gods?

Hooves on the ground sounded somewhere behind him, and the trickle dwindled to nothingness. His spirit and hope deflated. This was it, then. He capped his waterskin, and stood slowly, deliberately looping the waterskin back over his neck and tucking it under his sling. He drew and cocked his pistol, but left his gun hanging by his side.

Heker's ears pricked backwards and he snorted a challenge as he turned. Tjety turned likewise. The dark man's pair of bandits moved through the trees, ducking under low branches. One had a pistol, the other a rifle. Tjety heard another horse somewhere behind them. Had to be the man in dark robes. He centered himself as best he could and drew on that little pool of fresh *hekau*, a precious gift from Hapi.

Before the two bandits had fully cleared the trees, Tjety focused his *hekau*, brought up his pistol, and placed two perfect shots into each of them. They toppled off their horses and fell onto the hard ground. With two bullets left, Tjety kept the gun up and focused his attention on the last rider coming out of the tree line.

The man in dark robes sat astride his black mare, holding the reins in one hand, with his other hand cocked on the pommel of his sheathed blade. His headcloth was looped around his mouth and neck. He offered an open-handed greeting and then lifted his hand to remove the folds of the headcloth from his face, revealing a white-toothed smile creasing a deeply tanned face. He had a thin black mustache and a regal, hooked nose.

"Well met, Ranger of the south."

Tjety kept his pistol aimed somewhere around the man's chest. "Give me one good reason I shouldn't shoot you dead right here and now."

The man's smile never wavered as he held his horse still in front of Tjety. "Despite recent events," he glanced at the two bodies to either side of him, "I have no quarrel with you. My House and your order have never encountered each other. Until now, anyway."

Tjety frowned. "You know my order but I don't know shit about yours."

The man smiled as he tucked loose folds of fabric back into his headcloth. "My house name would mean nothing to you, Ranger. We are neither Kekhmet nor Hesso. But as a form of introduction, my name is Zezago, Deshi of the House of Gintenka."

"Nice title, but it means fuck-all to me." Tjety's gun hand started to shake. "Why are you here?"

"Reasons well beyond your understanding."

Tjety's frown deepened. "All I know is your men sow destruction and discontent. You destroyed a village and caused many unnecessary deaths."

He licked his lips, uncertain how much longer he could hold up his gun. "I expect you're also responsible for the creation of those monstrous, unliving...things."

The smile on the man's face had broadened at each point, which made Tjety quail inside. The man flexed his hands, then after a moment staring at him, dismounted.

"I accept responsibility for all those things, and many more you can't possibly know." He stepped to the left of his horse and rested a hand on his sword's pommel again.

A bright flash from the man's *ba* told Tjety that the man had some skill with *hekau*, almost certainly stronger than his own. Tjety reached out and took hold of Heker's reins, and slowly started to sidestep toward the tree line. Zezago kept smiling and sidestepped as well, toward the river, countering Tjety's movements.

"What would you do, knowing that I am responsible for all those deaths?"

Tjety heard the mocking tone in the man's voice, and knew that this would not end well. In a burst of movement, he raised his pistol and fired his last two rounds.

Zezago's hand and sword were a blur of motion. Two metallic whines sounded in the air. In one explosion of *hekau* and muscle, the man had drawn his sword and somehow, *somehow*, deflected the two bullets.

By the gods, it's even possible the man had, insanely, cut them out of the gods-damned air!

Tjety stared awestruck through the gun smoke at Zezago, who brought his sword up to a ready position in a flick of steel shining in the sunlight. The man's back was to the river, and he stood ready, inviting him to attack him in the old ways, blade to blade.

Fuck that!

Tjety focused all his will and intent, and plunged into the very last vestiges of his *hekau* to create a virtual fist that extended to the dark man and punched him right off his feet and into the river beyond, his sword spinning out of his grip.

Tjety had clearly taken the man by surprise. As he sagged to his knees in the wet sand, he realized that he had even surprised himself. He'd only ever attempted a *hekau'druh* twice before, once in training and once during that screwed-up encounter in that fucking Kesh cantina. The very encounter that had gotten him exiled to this gods-damned frontier.

"Zezago's hand and sword were a blur of motion.
Two metallic whines sounded in the air."

He stared numbly as Zezago tumbled downstream. The man would be out of action for a while, but he'd get to the shore soon enough. Tjety knew he had to get moving as soon as possible, but there was just nothing left in him. He blinked dully at the glittering waves, wondering if it'd be better to just sink into the cool water and let the Iteru carry him away. He dropped his chin to his chest and closed his eyes. "Whatever your will, mighty Hapi. May it be done."

After a long moment of silence, he heard a few small splashes and then Heker snorted and nudged his back. Tjety snapped back to the present. He shook the fog out of his head and reached up to grab double-handfuls of Heker's mane. "Gimme a hand up, boy."

Tjety bodily pulled himself up onto Heker's back and slumped heavily against his neck. He fished for the reins and missed the first time, but caught them on the second reach and gently pulled Heker's head around to move them toward the road once again.

He walked Heker past the two fallen bandits and then nudged his flank and got underway. With his mind flat and senses exhausted, Tjety's only thought other than navigating the road was: How in the name of Mayat was he going to stand up to a man who could deflect bullets out of the air with a fucking sword?

GODS DAMN IT! Stop the line, stop the line!"
Qebsenuf stood up in his saddle and cupped
his hands around his mouth. "Stop, I said!"

One of the soldiers on the other side of
the river raised a hand and repeated the order.
"Stop, stop!"

Qebsenuf clenched his reins in his hands and
watched another construct flail helplessly as the
river current took hold and swept it away, downriver
and out of sight. He shook his head. "Stupid things
weren't built to swim."

His men held back the constructs still on the
western shore. "How we gonna get them across,
boss Qeb?"

Qebsenuf scratched at his chin, feeling the
prickles of stubble. He glanced across the river and

called out to Teffu, one of his scouts. "How's the ford?"

Teffu yelled back, "Deeper than we expected but fine for horses and men as long as we move careful!"

Qebsenuf raised a hand in frustration. "Well, gods-damn it, that doesn't help me now!"

Teffu raised his hands in a helpless shrug. Qebsenuf turned toward the other soldiers on his side of the shore and thought hard. How was he going to get the rest of his men and the remaining constructs across the river? They'd lost four of them already.

He stared at the river, and at the men and the horses, and the constructs, and asked himself what the Master Deshi might do. He didn't know the man all that well, but knew that he seemed to have an answer for every problem placed before him.

He thought about the arrowhead Zezago had given him, but no. This was not the time to use it. Zezago would view the cry for help as weakness and would not hesitate to punish him again, even kill him this time. Qebsenuf still wasn't quite sure how he had managed to live through their last exchange.

He shook his head. Master Deshi was testing him, and he had to pass this one. He'd pledged his service and his life to Zezago, and he could not, *would not*, fail him as Meret and the others had. No, there had to be a solution here.

Qebsenuf waved over one of his cleverer Hesso scouts. "Merlom, we have a problem. Help me reason this out."

Merlom nudged his mount over to Qebsenuf. "As I'm able, boss."

"We have a deeper river ford than expected, fifteen men, fifteen horses, and almost thirty constructs. We've lost four to the river current and have no time to recover them." He pointed to each item in turn. "How do we get everyone across so that we can get on the gods-damned trail to Fort Sekhmet?"

Merlom focused along with Qebsenuf. "Maybe…set up a bridge with two lengths of rope? Walk them across?"

Qebsenuf shook his head. "Easy enough for men, but these things can barely walk straight on solid ground. I wouldn't trust any of them to navigate a rope bridge."

Merlom frowned. "Hmm, well then."

Qebsenuf stared at the horses, a glimmer of an idea forming. "What if we rode double? One man and one construct per horse? Ride them across the water rather than pushing them through?"

"Ride with those things? Boss, I know you ain't crazy, but that idea sure makes me wonder."

"I think it's worth a try, don't you?"

"I guess, but I sure don't want to ride with one of those things. If you don't think they can manage a rope bridge, what makes you think they can mount a horse? Besides, the damn things are fragile. They're liable to fall apart from the bouncing in the saddle."

Qebsenuf frowned. "No, I think this is our only option. We can't go back the way we came, and there's no other workable crossing for miles. We can't build a bridge, and I think you're right—the rope bridge is a bad idea." He considered the variables, then nodded. "No, the only way is to get them on the horses."

He heeled his horse forward and gestured for the men on his side of the river to close in around him. Once they did, he raised his voice. "We need to get those constructs onto the other side of the river, and we have no time for alternatives or argument. We're going to take one construct each on our horses, ride them across, and then come back for more until all of them are safe on the other side."

He stared into each of their surprised gazes, forcing steel into his gaze and iron into his words. "We have to do this, or we won't be able to support Master Deshi. If any of you don't want to do this, then ford the river and hand off your horse to someone who will. I need your help, one way or the other."

The men arrayed around him traded looks, and he could tell they weren't happy. He glanced up at the sun, past noon now. "We need to get moving, so get on it. Do your best to carefully get them up on your horse, then ford the river and deposit them on the far side. Move, now."

Slowly, in ones and twos, the soldiers moved their horses toward the still line of constructs. Qebsenuf called out to them. "You're going to be pulled up onto the horses and ridden across the river. Don't move and don't struggle."

The constructs stared at him with their strange unblinking eyes. He pressed his hand against his chest, onto his Apep tattoo underneath his tunic. "Great lord Apep, help us get these things across the river. In your service, so be it."

He stood his horse off to one side and watched as his men gingerly figured out how to lift a construct onto the front of their saddles, and awkwardly balance them there before walking their horses through the river ford. The men already on the other side of the river waited with outstretched hands to support the horses and constructs as they reached the other side.

Merlom waited his turn to carry one across and glanced at him. "This has to be the most fuckin' ridiculous river crossing I've ever seen."

Qebsenuf nodded, but offered him a sidelong smile. "It's a damned strange sight, but it's working. I think Master Deshi would be pleased."

Merlom just shook his head and then rode forward to pull a construct up onto his horse.

Qebsenuf stared up at the sun. Even with this delay they had made good time. He focused on his troops and constructs again. It'd take time to get all the constructs across the river, and they might lose another one or two, but they were getting it done. Soon he'd be able to lead these men and these things onward.

"Where there's a will, there's a way," he muttered. Damned strange way to go, but he'd take it. For the Master Deshi, he'd have carried the damn things across the river on his own back.

ACOOL BREEZE RIPPLED across the
Iteru and shuddered the branches all around
as Ruia refilled a waterskin. If she hadn't
been leading the remains of her village for survival,
she might have thought it was a pretty day. "Doubt
we'll ever see another pretty day," she muttered.

One of the younger boys, Henturu, jogged up
the river shore toward her. "Ruia! Ruia! The bridge
is ahead!"

She stood up, a glimmer of hope kindling
in her breast. She stood and pressed her hands
to the small of her back to stretch it out. "How
close, Henturu?"

He leaned over to catch his breath, supporting
himself on a length of stick he had picked up from
somewhere along the way. She was amused to note

that it didn't look all that different from the length of wood she had used to fashion a spear the other day.

"Maybe twenty minutes? I ran real fast."

She smiled, in spite of her weariness. "I bet you did. Twenty minutes, huh?" So it wouldn't take long for the wagon and the rest of the survivors to get there. And that meant that she had to be ready to face down Setesk and his friends.

She rested a hand on Henturu's shoulder. "Thank you for running as fast as you did. You've been a big help."

He beamed at her as she knew he would. She added, "Go on, run to the wagon and get something to eat and drink. I'm sure you're hungry!"

Henturu nodded and then tore off along the shoreline, swinging his stick at the tall reeds as he passed by.

Ruia slung her waterskin around her shoulder and then trudged toward the wagon. She was sore from sitting on the bench all day, and she dreaded getting back onto that seat. She really just wanted to stretch out in the back of the wagon and sleep, though some part of her knew that she didn't have such an option. She pushed through the thin undergrowth and regained the clear road. She hurried the short distance to where the wagon and the other villagers were slowly trudging their way toward the crossroads.

Henturu had already reached them and was perched heroically on the wagon bench next to Aniba, a mealy apple in one hand and a bottle of water in the other. Some of the villagers were patting Henturu on the back or leg, wherever they could reach.

As Ruia walked up, he smiled. "I told everyone about the bridge!"

"I'm glad, Henturu." She caught a warning look from Aniba.

Setesk stepped around the wagon with his three allies arrayed around him. They all had their rifles in hand, and while they weren't actually aimed at her, they certainly seemed to be in an aggressive posture. "If the bridge is up ahead, means the crossroads is too."

Ruia nodded. "That's right."

Setesk stopped several paces from her. "And that means we'll be getting on toward the village."

Ruia settled her gaze on him. She raised her voice and hoped that everyone would hear.

"We cross the bridge and make for the fort." She pointed into the sky. "It's well after noon. We have maybe five hours of workable light left to us. If we push hard, we can reach the fort late tonight."

"No, ma'am." Setesk called out. "No, we ride for home and leave the bridge and that fool Ranger behind."

Mutters of agreement sounded from his three allies. Ruia was somewhat heartened to hear no responses from the others. She suspected they were keeping silent, waiting to see how this would all play out.

Ruia willed her heart to steady its rushing beats. She tried consciously pulling some strength from her *hekau* and felt the drain, but it was soon replaced by a rush of confidence. Strange. She'd have to ask Tjety about it later, if there was a later.

She shook her head. "We're not going to risk all of these people. There is nothing left for us at the village but more death. We're going to the fort, and that's all I have to say about that."

Setesk glanced at his allies, then swept his gaze over the other villagers. "Friends, listen to me. We've come this far and now it's time to go home. I appreciate what Ruia has done for us, but now it's time for her to get some rest. Let me lead you home."

Ruia yelled out. "And you listen to me! Go with this man if you want but leave the rest of us to go to the fort. We don't have time to stand here and argue about this!"

Setesk shook his head and gestured toward her vaguely with his rifle. "We stick together. That's the way it has to be."

"No, damn you." Somehow the pistol slung around her chest appeared in her right hand, aimed at Setesk's heart. How had that happened? She didn't remember drawing it. She felt renewed strength through her *hekau*, rushing cold blood into her veins and forging steel in her eyes.

Setesk stared down the barrel at her. "You ain't gonna shoot me." He offered a hesitant laugh. "We got enough wounded and dead as it is."

She cocked the pistol with a firm motion of her thumb. "We're going over the bridge together, Setesk. With or without you."

He licked his dry lips, and glanced from villager to villager, looking for support but finding none. His hands tensed on his rifle. "I ain't gonna…"

Ruia's pistol leapt in her hand, the crack of the gunshot sounding loud in the afternoon air. With wide eyes, she stared at Setesk through the gun smoke. Had she really shot him?

Setesk blinked at her several times, mouth agape.

"Somehow the pistol slung around Ruia's chest appeared in her right hand, aimed at Setesk's heart."

He stuttered out, "I...I..."

She cocked back the hammer again. "We're going over the bridge." She didn't trust herself to say anything more.

He continued to stare at her as a thin puddle expanded around his feet. "I...heard the bullet pass my ear." He glanced down and then turned an impressive shade of red. "Aw, shit."

She gestured toward the nearby river with the pistol barrel. "Best clean yourself before we move on."

He blinked a few more times, then handed his rifle off to one of his silent allies, and gingerly stepped out of the puddle he'd formed.

As Setesk walked away, she lowered her pistol and fixed each remaining villager with a stare. "If you don't trust yourselves, then trust in me. I'll get us to the fort. I promise you that." She gestured toward the crossroads. "Any damn fool who wants to walk to the village is welcome to do so. The rest of us are crossing the river."

The villagers traded looks with each other and then started walking toward the crossroads and the long wooden bridge built on stone foundations just beyond.

Ruia glanced at Aniba. "Let's get moving." She

glanced at the pistol in her hand, uncocked it, and then set it back into the holster slung across her chest. She tried hard not to think about how its presence and weight comforted her.

Aniba stared at her as she returned to her seat on the bench. "Thought you was gonna shoot him for sure."

The truth spilled out of her before she could stop it. "I…think I meant to. Must have flinched at the last." She blinked in surprise.

Aniba's eyes widened. "Gods, Ruia. You're turning into a hard woman. Bless your *ba*. Your ma and da would be proud."

She simply nodded, not trusting herself to respond. *Was* she turning hard? She furrowed her brow. Would she have shot Setesk? She barely registered her friends as they walked alongside the wagon—some offered her smiles while others just stared at her with what she guessed was either confusion or fear in their faces. Setesk shuffled along behind the wagon, eyes downcast.

She wondered what Tjety might have done, but the strangely comfortable chill in her heart told her all she needed to know.

THE SUN WAS EDGING down toward the western mountains when Tjety pulled up rein at the long wooden bridge spanning the Iteru. He'd pushed Heker hard initially after leaving the dark man behind, but had eased off since then, knowing he had to conserve his mount's strength. He wiped his brow with his dirty tunic sleeve. The fever he'd felt earlier hadn't eased off; in fact, he felt like his head was encased in thick wool.

"Gotta keep moving, friend," he said, as he reached down and rubbed Heker's neck. "Hope you're feeling up to a fresh rider." An idea had been forming in his mind, and the more he replayed it, and the more he struggled to keep the sense of it together in his fever-fogged state, the more it made sense.

He glanced at the tracks in the dirt once he and Heker reached the eastern side of the bridge, but didn't bother tapping into his *hekau* to help interpret the tracks. He had nothing left. "Wagon can't be too far ahead, so let's keep at it."

He was talking to himself as much as to Heker—whatever it took to keep focus on the trail ahead. He'd glanced back frequently, checking for pursuit, but so far nothing had materialized. He was sure it was coming, though. That dark man, that Zezago—he didn't seem like the retiring type.

He put heel to Heker again and trotted over the bridge, Heker's hooves clopping on the old wooden slats. Once he was back on solid ground, Tjety spared a few precious moments for his mount to drink from the river, then pushed him back onto the road and into a steady pace.

Time seemed to be less important as he worked along the trail, the steady stream of trees and grass rolling past blurring into one long haze. In a moment of rational thought, he realized that the fever had to be taking hold, and forced himself upright on Heker's back.

He glanced up at the setting sun. "Amun-Re, oh mighty and divine, if you could look upon this humble servant and offer a little fucking assistance, it'd be sorely appreciated." He glanced at the shimmering road in front of his eyes, blinked hard, then added, "Just get me to the wagon. Just that far."

He didn't get an answer, or even a twinge from his *hekau*, but some point after his entreaty he thought he saw a human form materialize on the path ahead. He steered Heker toward that vision with his knees, realizing that his head had sagged down to his chest and was only just above Heker's ears.

"Ranger? Hey, Ranger!"

Tjety felt his left leg shake, and he roused himself out of his stupor. One of the villager boys was tugging at his kilt. Somehow, his feverish mind came up with the boy's name. "Moser, right?"

The kid nodded, his short sidelock flopping. "That's me! You remembered my name!"

Tjety raised a hand to quell Moser's excitement. "Help me get to the wagon."

Moser nodded excitedly, and pointed up the road. "It's just ahead. Ruia'll be happy to see you! She nearly shot Setesk!" He grinned and then ran away from him, paused, and then ran back to him. "I forgot to lead you. Come on!" He reached out for Heker's reins and pulled his head toward the direction of the wagon.

Tjety helped by giving Heker a little heel, but otherwise let Moser set the pace. Heker was easy enough to lead and was confident being led with him on his back.

True to Moser's word, the wagon was just ahead, loaded down with villagers. Ruia and Aniba were seated on the bench, and the remaining twenty or so villagers walked along, some ahead of the wagon and to either side. A sad caravan of people struggling to find safety.

Moser called out. "Ruia! The Ranger has returned!"

Most of the villagers perked up at that, and turned curious eyes toward him and Heker. Ruia started, and turned to face him. She stood as Moser led Heker over to the wagon.

"As the sun is my witness, you look like shit, Tjety."

He offered a wan smile and nudged Heker over to the wagon, and pulled his leg over his horse's neck and stepped into the wagon bed, barely missing stumbling on one of the sleeping crones. Matti, maybe, or Gheti. He couldn't tell them apart.

He stood on unsteady feet and massaged his arm just below the bloodstained bandage. "I've been better."

She stared at him, then glanced down the road behind them. "Where are Mut and Yufa? Khepri?"

Tjety met her eyes and simply shook his head. "Our enemy caught up to us. Khepri and the others, they fought hard and dished out as good as they got, but they're all dead. I'm sorry, Ruia." He glanced at the others. "I'm sorry for us all. We did the best we could."

He sighed, rubbed his blazing arm wound again. "And I faced off against their leader, a dark man in dark robes. With a sword. He was fierce."

One of the villagers, Sefer, helped him to a sitting spot in the wagon bed. "What happened?"

Tjety gratefully took a waterskin pressed into his hands and drank greedily, not caring that he spilled half of it on his tunic. "The leader and four of his men caught up to us in the road. Mut's horse had come up lame. There was a brisk fight and in seconds, Mut, Khepri, Yufa, and two of the bandits were all shot down. I managed to get farther down the road, but they caught up to me. I killed the other two bandits, and then dug deep and surprised their leader with an old Ranger trick."

He glanced at Ruia. "It's a *hekau* thing. Remind me to teach it to you someday." He drained the waterskin. "Anyways, I pushed that son-of-a-bitch into the water and then somehow managed to get back on Heker's back and rode hard to meet up with you. Once I saw the crossroads, I guessed that you had to have crossed the bridge." He focused on Ruia again. "Good on you for sticking to the plan."

Ruia shrugged. "It wasn't as easy as that, but here we are."

Tjety glanced at Aniba. "Best keep the wagon moving."

Aniba nodded, then turned back to his driving and slapped the leads to get the horses moving again. Most of the villagers clustered around the wagon and kept pace. Ruia stepped over the wagon bench and settled down next to Tjety.

"How are you feeling?"

Tjety indicated his arm. "This thing is infected. And I'm feverish—not seeing so well either. I had to step off Heker for fear of falling off." He focused on her. "What's this I hear about you almost shooting Setesk?"

Ruia touched the pistol hanging from the holster slung across her chest, then lifted her hand to clasp her amulet. "We had a difference of opinion and I had to…make my point."

"So you almost shot him?"

She shrugged. "It got his attention."

"Say more." He leaned back against the wagon's side and grabbed another waterskin from the stack among the sleeping bodies.

She shifted so that she sat cross-legged in front of him and tucked her filthy dress around her legs. "Setesk's been antsy all day, and got up the courage to try and take charge when we reached the crossroads. I told him our best chance was to head to the fort, but he and his friends wanted to return home."

She stared off toward Setesk, who trailed behind the wagon, looking downcast. "He didn't exactly threaten me, but we traded harsh words and in a moment, I had my pistol in my hand and aimed at his heart. I even pulled the trigger, but something made me miss."

He focused on her as she talked. "And what was that?"

She looked away and then met his eyes. "I don't know. My *hekau*? A whiff of a breeze? The Lady Mayat?" She shrugged. "Anyways. I didn't hit him but it was enough to get him to back off. The villagers trust me and my lead, and I think he will too. Assuming we get to the fort."

He sighed. "I don't think I'm going to be a whole lot of help to you, Ruia. This fever's kicking me hard and I've got to get some rest."

She placed a hand on one of his leather greaves. "What can I do?"

Tjety closed his eyes, started to drift off, but then rallied and focused on her again. "Take Heker and ride as hard and as fast as you can to Fort Sekhmet."

Ruia stared into his eyes and lowered her voice to keep the other villagers from hearing. "Are you sure that's a good idea? What if something happens to you while I'm gone?"

He tried a smile, but didn't really feel it. "It's a big risk but we don't have another option. I don't dare ride there myself and leave you and the others alone. If I can get some rest, they need my gun more than my speed."

"You said yourself that you're not feeling well. Your gun won't be much good if you're flat on your back with a fever."

Tjety pursed his lips. "Good point. If you ever pursue Ranger training, you'll have the trainers running around in circles trying to keep up with you." He offered a weak smile. "But, there are times when you are given orders and need to follow them."

She frowned. "Is this one of those times?"

He opened his mouth, then closed it again. "Of course not. You're not a Ranger so I can't order you around." He glanced at the villagers as they walked along, ignoring the curious looks they were shooting toward him and Ruia.

"But, I can ask this of you and let you be the one to decide what happens next." He shifted his arm. "I am badly wounded. I can't ride. I can barely shoot, and I need rest." He took a deep breath and continued. "I can keep us moving toward the fort, and I can use my pistol or khopesh in close fighting if needed, especially if I can get a couple hours' rest and maybe something to eat."

Tjety indicated Heker, walking alongside the wagon. "You told me you're a better rider than most of the surviving villagers and I'm going to guess you've gotten a little more rest than I have." He leaned in close. "And you're the only one here I'd trust to get a message to the fort."

She inclined her head. "How do I convince the fort's commander to help us?"

He reached over and pulled his satchel off Heker's back. "I'll write a short letter and give you my headcloth. If the letter doesn't convince him, I hope to the lowest depths of the Duat that my headcloth will tip the balance. You tell him a fucking Ranger doing Pharaoh's fucking service is in need of his help. He should come running with his troops." He scratched at his stubble. "At least I hope so. I've never been this far north. Some fort captains are shifty and have thoughts of their own."

"Gods, Tjety, I don't know." She shook her head. "I've only been to the fort once, to help my da trade fish for supplies. I think I heard him say that the fort captain used to spend a lot of time in the governor's palace, but that was just after the fort was established and the troops moved in."

"Hmm, all right. They might have just been communicating troop movements for the frontier. Any idea how often the fort sent out troops on patrol?"

She shrugged. "I don't know if they ever did. Or if they did, they never made it as far as our village."

He frowned at that, wishing he had paid more attention to the scouting reports at the Asyut garrison. "These frontier companies were supposed to protect all the villages under their province's domain." He sighed. "But, I'll get that letter written now. Better than nothing."

He hunkered down on the floor of wagon and set up a space to use as a writing surface. He pulled pen and papyrus and ink out of his satchel, and balanced the inkwell on his knee. He dipped the pen into the inkwell and began to write in short, jerky letters. It took him a few minutes and a few curses and scratched-out words thanks to the bouncing wagon, but soon enough his short missive was complete. He blew on the ink to help it set, then plugged up the inkwell and waved the sheet of papyrus in the air to dry the ink.

Tjety glanced at Ruia. "All right, best you mount Heker now."

"I still haven't said I'm going yet."

He let out a burst of air in exasperation. "Do you need me to fuckin' say please?"

She shrugged. "Would it kill you?"

He caught the glimmer of a smile on her face and the twinkle of mischief in her eyes, one that he remembered seeing in his own in earlier, better days.

He took a deep breath, let it out, then looked her in the eyes. Gods, she had a strong spirit. "Ruia, would you be willing to take this letter and my headcloth to the company commander at Fort Sekhmet and formally ask for his assistance in getting us all back to the fort before we all fucking die?" He paused for a heartbeat, and realized he'd forgotten the word. He hastily added, "Please."

She stared at him for a heartbeat or two, then smiled. "I will, thank you, Tjety." She reached over for Heker's reins and shifted herself from the wagon and onto his back. She reached out for the letter.

Tjety folded it twice and then handed it to her. He untied his headcloth sling and stretched out the length of it, folded it down to a more portable size, and then handed it to her with reverence.

"Please take good care of this. I've had it for nearly three years and it is the most important thing to me next to my pistol and my khopesh." He blinked, surprised at himself for admitting as much. *Fucking Mayat. You've got me trusting in you all over again.*

She nodded, but looked confused. She accepted the folded headcloth and tucked it into her satchel. "I'll keep it safe, Tjety."

He nodded. "Thank you. Now, while you still have light, ride, Ruia. Ride as if all the slithering minions of Apep were at your heels."

She gathered up the reins and then without another word, nodded and wheeled Heker away and put heel to him. She rode off, following the road into the trees. Villagers stared at her as she went by. Some turned back to glance at him, but most of them focused on the road ahead and on putting one foot in front of the other.

Tjety massaged his hurt arm and tried to place himself into the footsteps of these people. He couldn't imagine what they must be thinking, the enormity of what they had gone through over the past few days.

He thought he had it rough—exiled to the frontier with just his horse for company, getting into a firefight with Meret and his goons, the chase along the trail, the earthquake that couldn't have been just an earthquake, getting shot and then beaten up, the battle around the camp fighting for freedom, and then the long running fight to end up here. These were the most trying days he'd experienced thus far, and yet they had to pale in comparison to what the villagers had faced.

They had lost their village, their friends and family, even their very livelihood. They had nothing left in all the world except each other, and they largely had one young girl to thank for what they did have. He had played a small part in their escape and freedom, but Ruia deserved the larger share of the credit.

He settled into the wagon and found a strip of linen to use as a replacement sling. Once his wounded arm was tucked tight against his chest, he laid back and focused on the others. The villagers were quiet—no banter traded, no kind words or even harsh words shared. Just dogged determination to take a step, then another. The sleeping and the wounded in the wagon with him were quiet save for a few soft groans of pain. A couple of the children clung to each other and wept quietly. One of the two old sisters knitted strands of separated rope into fishing nets, her fingers never slowing.

Tjety glanced behind the wagon. No sign of the dark man, Zezago, or his troops. He thought he had taken out all of the man's allies, but of course he couldn't be sure. The man was resourceful and cunning, and it was entirely possible he had more minions spread across the countryside looking for the remnants of the villagers. There could be an enemy behind every tree.

Tjety tamped down a swelling of panic and tried to reach within for a little strength from his *hekau*, but there was nothing left. His vision grayed over and he rested his head on the thighs of another sleeping man, trying to wedge himself against the wagon's side and the other warm bodies to find a workable position to get some rest.

He stared up at Aniba's back. "Driver, for all the gods' sake, keep us moving."

Aniba glanced back at him, nodded, then turned back and snapped the reins to get the horses moving a little faster. The wagon lurched under Tjety's body. He closed his eyes and tried to start the mental repetitions of the litany he'd been taught, the spell designed to bring rest to the body and restoration to the *ba* and *hekau*. He wished he had something to eat, and made a point to drain the waterskin in his hand. For any hope of his body to heal and to fight the infection crashing into his body, he'd need richer sustenance, but didn't know if or when that would come.

He feared it would come too late.

12

COLD WATER SLITHERING UP his nose roused Zezago, and he opened his eyes to find his face pressed against wet sand. He inhaled automatically and sat up, coughing out the cold liquid. He leaned over and coughed more, clearing his lungs and head.

He was on his hands and knees in the muck along the western shore of the Iteru. He must have drifted downriver after that Ranger had knocked him back and into the water. He whipped his head back and forth, sending more droplets flying. He pushed himself to his feet and took a few tentative steps up the shoreline and onto dry land.

In the waning sunlight, Zezago took a quick inventory. Headcloth on but tangled around his head and neck. He pulled it off and wrung it out as best he could, then loosely draped it around his neck and shoulders. It'd have to dry before he could re-wrap it. His scabbard was still attached to the belt, but there was no sign of his sword. He tamped down a sudden surge of anxiety about that, and started to walk north along the shore, casting out with his *hekau* for the blade. He had set a location charm into the pommel of the blade long ago, which had proved useful in more than one battle.

He shook water out of his ears as he walked, his sandals squishing. The Ranger had been a surprise to him from the very start of the engagement. That he had favored the pistol over the sword was disappointing, though not surprising. He shouldn't have expected much from a Kekhmet heathen. The old ways, the honorable ways, were a dying art. He felt a pang of sorrow for the turning of the world. Things had been so easier, so much more honest, before guns and machines and the strange new *hekau* known as technology.

His own natural *hekau*, the true way, pinged in his mind as he got a read on his blade. He moved a few more steps up the river, and then waded into the chilly waters and fished around the sandy river bed. He had to take a breath and dive before he wrapped his hand around the leather grip and surfaced.

Zezago took a deep gulp of air and then waded back to shore with the blade held high. He shook water out of his ears again, and flicked the blade to clear it of most of the water. Using his sodden clothing to dry it would be useless. He sheathed the blade, making a mental note to tend to it as soon as he could. He glanced at the river in distaste. There weren't such large rivers in his homeland. Traveling over or on this one was a necessary evil of invading Kekhmet, at least until he could secure other means of entry into the broken empire.

He glanced up and down the shore as far as he could see in the growing dusk, and then whistled a sharp tune. He paused to listen, then whistled again. After a moment, a whinny sounded from farther north along the river and then the sound of hooves on the ground reached his ears.

Soon enough, his beloved mare, Kubela, came into view, trotting along the river toward him. Her mane and tail looked matted, as if she'd been trudging through the brambles and briars along the tree line. Her legs from hoof to shoulder were matted down with water and her nose and chin were still dripping.

Zezago reached out to take hold of the reins and gently pulled his mount's head down to scratch her between the ears, on her tiny white mark in the shape of a crescent moon. "You foolish thing. What have you gotten yourself into?"

He held onto Kubela's bridle and reached up to comb his long fingers through her long, supple mane, but they got tangled up on brambles and other bits of debris. He bumped his forehead against her cheek. "Don't have time to clean you up now, my girl. It'll have to wait."

Kubela whuffled and nudged him with her nose. Zezago patted her nose again, and then stepped up into the saddle and settled on her back. "Flattery will do you no good right now. There's much to do."

He pulled Kubela's head around to the north and got her walking, then trotting. He found a break in the trees and went through it to return to the old trader's road. He followed the road north for a few minutes, lamenting the lost time chasing after that Ranger and the remnants of the villagers, but knew it was necessary. He had to see to his fallen servants.

The first body appeared in the darkening light just ahead on the road, several more sprawled out on the road behind. He dismounted and secured the reins to the saddle pommel, leaving Kubela to graze. He approached the first body, which turned out to be one of the villagers.

He stood over the body for a few moments, surprised to feel a vestige of respect for the man. To fight so hard against an enemy you didn't know and who had decimated your village…impressive. He knelt down to better examine the body. This one had been taken down by a gunshot to the chest. He reached down and tore open the man's shirt, then pushed up his own sleeves and plunged a finger into the ragged hole in the man's chest.

Zezago poked and prodded the wound, ignoring the thickening blood leaking out and around his fingers and hands. The bullet had chipped a rib and then caromed into the man's heart. A good shot made better by a fortuitous ricochet. He pulled out his small knife and made two neat incisions, then put the knife aside. He took a deep breath, focused his *hekau*, and then with a whispered litany tore the man's chest open with his bare hands, pulling muscle and sinew apart to expose the rib cage.

Then, grabbing a long rib in each hand, he flexed them until he had enough room to reach in and grab the soggy meat that remained of the heart. He held the bloody mass of flesh with one hand as he took his knife and then worked it inside the man's chest to detach the grisly prize from its housings. With one last cut through the thin flesh, the broken heart came free. Zezago raised it up to his eyes critically, taking in the tubes and chambers that had been violated by the bullet.

Once he'd seen all he wanted to see, he unceremoniously tossed the heart aside. It landed in the dirt with a wet splat. He reached into the satchel slung over his shoulder and rummaged around for a heart scarab. He wiped what blood he could off his hands and onto the limestone scarab, doing his best to coat all sides of the thing with the brownish fluid. He rested one hand on the body and cupped the scarab in his hand, and closed his eyes.

Uttering the ancient words of his House, he tapped into the deep reservoir of *hekau* contained within his *ba* and flowed a stream of arcane energies into the matrix he'd developed within the limestone scarab, activating its charges and pathways. He felt the drain from the core of his being, the issuance of personal power almost an orgasmic release. Zezago controlled his breathing as he worked the spell, and then with a final push, closed off the *hekau* flow from his *ba* to the scarab.

He worked a simple leather thong through the small hole drilled into the scarab and then with both hands shoved the scarab into the body's open chest cavity, and with nimble fingerwork, tied the thong securely to what remained of the body's spine. He pulled his hands out and rested them both on the ribcage.

He began the closing litany, and cried out the closing verse. "And as your sunset becomes a new sunrise, awaken to your new life and new prosperity!"

He shot a surge of *hekau* into the scarab, activating the scarab's intent. The body convulsed under his hands and then shook a couple times, a new life flowing into its limbs.

The man's eyes, half-lidded in death, snapped open, and rapidly took on an iridescent green glow that started dim then brightened. Zezago smiled down at his creation, and then stood up. The newly-made construct stared up into the sky, as if taking stock of its new essence, then looked at him with its new eyes.

"Rise, my son. Rise, and do as I bid you."

Zezago held his hands out to either side as the

construct, somewhat awkward in its new form, got to its unsteady feet. He smiled at it again, then gestured toward the other bodies down the road. "Bring the three largest bodies to me. I have to create some fellows for you."

The new construct simply turned and shuffled toward the other bodies strewn out on the path. The Ranger and his allies had fought hard, as had the troops that had ridden with him from the quarry. Some of the bodies left on the road would be fortunate enough to serve him in a new form and a new life. If there was a more generous gift he could have given them, he didn't know of it.

He knelt down on the road near the drying pool of blood that had been the man's life, and pulled the three remaining scarabs out of his satchel. There were more than three bodies on the road, but he had the means to build just three more constructs.

He regretted the loss of additional raw materials, the bodies he'd leave behind, but there was nothing to be done for it. The wooden amulets he had experimented with just could not hold enough *hekau* to be effective. He suspected it had something to do with the natural life-energy the trees themselves created, but he wasn't enough of a theoretical practitioner to know.

As it was, he found limestone to be among the better resources for his work, even though he suspected that there had to be something better. The constructs he built using the limestone scarabs were generally effective for the uses he needed them for, but more and more he was finding that he needed living slaves to do more work. He needed more time to study and to experiment, and more materials to experiment with.

His new construct reached down and started dragging another body, one that had been a woman, toward him. Zezago rested his hands on his knees and reached inward to gather up more of his *hekau*. He'd bring three more children into this new world and then he'd get back on the hunt for the Ranger and his remaining allies.

As he finished building his new children, hooves on the road to the north sounded and he focused on them as he stood, his robe sleeves pushed high up on his arms and his hands covered in gore. One of his men, a sergeant whose name he didn't recall, rode close and wheeled around, his horse clearly spooked at the blood.

"Master Deshi! We've been looking for you for more than an hour, and…"

Zezago raised his hands. "No matter, sergeant. I am here, and as you can see, well enough." He dropped his hands to his side. More of his men rode into the area and paused to stretch saddle-weary legs or to pass a waterskin or flask among themselves.

Zezago focused on the sergeant. "See that the men water their horses and eat something quick. As soon as I am clean, we ride hard. The Ranger and his allies cannot be far ahead."

The sergeant nodded and moved over to the men to relay the orders. Zezago took one last look at his new creations, then moved toward the river to wash away the gore. He glanced at the setting sun. He would face that Ranger in battle again soon.

RUIA RODE HARD WELL into the moonrise. Every time she stopped Heker along the road for water and rest, she thought about turning around, but she had a feeling, she guessed it had to be through her *hekau*, that she needed to get to the fort quickly. Her people needed her, and she couldn't let them down after everything else that had happened.

She pushed east along the road, doubting herself at every mile marker. What if she was going the wrong way and somehow missed the fort in the dark?

She rolled that question around in her mind for a while as she prodded Heker along the road, spinning herself up into the worst-case scenarios—that she would miss the fort completely and end up lost in the deeper frontier, or worse, end up in Hesso territory and be captured and sold into their slave trade.

The comfortable sway of the amulet around her neck distracted her, and she realized that she was getting herself worked up for no good reason. She approached the problem piece by piece, as her ma had taught her. First, the simple evidence in front of her was that this road led directly to the old ruined sun temple the fort had been built near. As long as she kept to the road, she'd eventually come to the fort.

Second, a small town had been built up next to the fort, and people at night usually meant lights, even candlelight in windows or torches on a fence or lanterns lining the streets.

Third, and most simply, the Ranger had told her to follow the road to the fort, and that, if nothing else, should have been enough for her to know she was on the right track. 'Common gods-damned sense', as her brother Paneb might have said.

She took a gulp of water from her waterskin, smothering the thought of her brother, and then heeled Heker down the road.

She lost track of the time in the darkness, as a low bank of clouds moved in and partially obscured the moon. The shadows started to play tricks with her mind, and she pushed Heker harder, though she could feel him heaving under her legs and knew that he'd need to rest soon.

She felt strangely comfortable on Heker. Tjety rode bareback like her and most other Kekhmet riders. It was good she was comfortable on his back because it gave her one less thing to worry about. Every tree along the road looked like a threat about to leap out at her, every branch the arm of one of those unliving creatures that had attacked her village.

She saw a faint glow ahead through the trees, which grew in size and intensity as she rode closer. The tree line ended at the edge of a clear, narrow field, and a short distance beyond the treeline was the outline of a tall stone wall stretching out into the darkness. Farther in the distance, on a tall rise overlooking the fort, the town, and the field all around, loomed the ruined spire of an ancient sun temple. The road she followed paralleled the wall, so she followed them along, marveling anew at the sheer size and height of the fort's thick stone walls. She seemed to remember one of the village elders saying that the fort's walls had once been part of the sun temple complex.

As she moved along the road, a section of the wall sloped up and up into a massive pylon form, set against one side of the fort's closed wooden gates. Another massive pylon squatted on the other side of the gates, with another long stretch of stone wall beyond that.

Encouraged by the sight, she put her heels to Heker and urged him onward. "Come on, boy, just a little farther and we'll get you something to eat and drink."

He whuffled and pushed on under her command.

As she neared the gates, she saw movement on top of the walls. It was clear that she was being watched. She rode up to the gate, unable to stifle a feeling of awe at the massive stone pylons erected to either side of the tall wooden gates. The pylons were faced with unadorned plaster and seemed to glow in the moonlight. The walls themselves were likewise unadorned plaster, but there were places where the plaster had cracked or fallen away. She guessed that the pylons and the gates had been added to the much older walls.

She shook off the wonderment, remembering her task. Without waiting for someone to call down and challenge her, she yelled out. "In the name of the Rangers of Mayat and the pharaoh, open the gates!"

A face appeared out of one of the small wooden guard towers perched precariously atop the walls. "Ho, there! Did you say Rangers?"

She called up. "I did. I'm on Ranger business. Open your gates!"

The head lingered for a moment, then ducked out of view. She heard two whispered voices talk back and forth, but the muffled voices plus the intervening distance and walls between conspired to hide the words from her.

After what sounded like heated discussion, the face appeared again. "Hold there a moment. We'll open the gate."

The face disappeared from view again. Sounds of bodies moving over wood slats echoed in her ears, followed by the rhythmic sounds of feet falling on a wooden ladder. Whoever had been in that tower was coming down to ground level.

The footsteps padded over to the gates, and then the sound of several metal bolts being cranked open echoed in her ears.

Finally, one of the large gates slowly swung open toward her. The same face poked out from behind the gate, followed by an arm clad in a leather bracer and a short-sleeved military tunic. "Come in, come in. Hurry."

She heeled Heker forward and passed through the gate. The soldier, who didn't look much older than her, waited for her to pass before pulling it shut behind him.

She leaned forward and stretched her sore muscles. Once the guard locked the gate, he walked over with a long rifle in his hands. The curiosity on his face turned to suspicion when he got a good look at her in the fire light.

"Now I think you've been fooling me, miss. No offense intended, but I'm thinking you're far too young to be a Ranger." He looked her up and down. "Not unless things in the south are far worse than we know."

She shook her head at the question in his voice. "You're not wrong. I'm not actually a Ranger." She quickly rose a hand to show she meant no harm, and pulled Tjety's headcloth out of her satchel. "However, I'm here at a Ranger's request." She offered the bunched-up blue fabric to him.

The soldier stared at her and then raised his free hand as if to ward away the offering. "I don't know nothing about taking requests from Rangers. I think..."

She cleared her throat. "I think you need to take me to the captain."

Their exchange had attracted some attention, and she glanced to the side to see a pair of soldiers, one young and one old, pause in their travels to stare at them. The older one pushed the younger one on toward a long, narrow building. "Get yourself some sleep, Nefer. I'll be along directly to lock up."

The younger of the two soldiers nodded and headed toward the long building, giving her a couple curious looks before focusing on his destination.

The older soldier approached and waved toward the guard who had let her in through the gate. "Go on, Meritamun, go back to your post and keep a watchful eye out. I'll take her to the captain."

The gate guard took a step back and saluted the older man. "I'll leave her to you then, Sergeant." He turned to head back to his ladder and his tower.

The sergeant hooked his thumbs into his kilt belt and nodded at her. "Name's Sergeant Bennu, my dear, but you can just call me Bennu, or Old Bennu if you're feeling charitable." His eyes twinkled in the fire light over an impressive bushy beard with ample salt and pepper sprinkled throughout.

She offered him a tired smile, his tone and demeanor making him instantly likable. "Thank you, Bennu. I'm Ruia."

He nodded at the bunch of blue fabric in her hands. "Unless my eyes deceive me, that there is a Ranger headcloth." He looked at her with curiosity clear on his face.

She offered the headcloth to him. "It is. A Ranger gave it to me and asked me to bring it here, with a message. He indicated that it would be sufficient for me to gain access to the fort, and, if needed, the fort's captain."

Bennu held up a hand to refuse the headcloth. "Hold onto that. I'll take you to the captain." He indicated which direction to walk down the main thoroughfare through the fort and town, and fell into step next to her.

Ruia tried to focus on the steps ahead, but everywhere she looked were one- and two-story buildings made of a mix of stone, wood, and mudbrick, with garishly painted doors, windows with what appeared to be real glass, and signs everywhere touting wares from fishhooks to baths.

She hadn't been to the town in years, and the place was foreign and intimidating. Nothing like her humble little village.

He glanced sidelong at her as they walked. "You're clearly not a townie, Ruia. Mayhap you're from one of the fishing villages nearby?"

She nodded. "My village is to the south, beyond the bridge and the crossroads. Or was, anyway."

When he offered her a questioning look, she added, "We were attacked and wiped out by bandits. There's hardly any of us left."

Bennu stopped her in the street. "Attacked? When?" His eyes seemed to express genuine concern.

"Two mornings ago, I guess. Maybe three? I've lost count."

"Oh, gods. I had no idea. Come on!" He grabbed her arm above the elbow and pulled her toward several small one-room mudbrick homes lined up alongside the thoroughfare. One was slightly larger than the others, and the military pennant planted outside of it on a stout pole painted gold suggested it had to be the captain's home.

Bennu said, "We've been on patrols to the north the last couple weeks. The new captain intended to get to the southern villages next."

He brought her to the closed door of the larger house, and rapped on the door with his free hand. There was no response from the first knock, so he tried again and then called out as well. "Captain? It's Sergeant Bennu. We have a situation, sir."

Muffled sounds reached her from inside the house, and then a man coughed a few times and then shuffled over to the door. A bolt was thrown, and then the wooden door opened and swung inside.

A youngish man peered out. His short dark hair was rumpled and he was buckling on a drab military-cut kilt over his nakedness. He blinked bleary eyes at the torchlight and squinted alternately at her and at Bennu. "Sergeant, what's this all about? Not another runaway seeking escape from Madame Teteri's?"

Bennu shook his head. "No, sir. This one's name is Ruia. Say's she's here at the bequest of a Ranger."

She offered Tjety's headcloth and letter to the captain. "It's urgent, captain. Our village was attacked a couple days ago and the Ranger was there to help us, but..."

The captain stared at the headcloth as if it were a snake that might leap out and strike him. He retreated a step into his home. "I'm sorry, we can't get involved in Ranger business." He glanced at

Bennu. "See that she and her horse are adequately provisioned and then send her on her way."

Bennu and Ruia traded a look, then Bennu focused on the captain. "With respect, sir, shouldn't we at least hear her out? Her village was attacked, people killed…"

The captain glanced at her again, then at the headcloth, and then back to Bennu. "I made myself clear, sergeant. Or at least I hope I did. Give her some food and water, and get her out of here. We are not about to involve ourselves with Ranger business. We have our own battles to face."

The captain shook his head. Something, maybe her *hekau*, helped her sense fear behind his eyes. "I am sorry for your troubles and for the plight of your village. If you have a complaint to lodge, I entreat you to approach the provincial governor's court. He will hear your concerns in due course and, if warranted, will send the army to investigate." He glanced at Bennu. "Sergeant, dismissed."

Bennu opened his mouth, but the captain stepped back into his quarters and shut the door on them. Ruia heard the wooden bolt snap home inside the door, the sound offering hollow finality to her feelings of despair.

She blinked a few times, the despair in her soul at odds with the rage building inside her. Without another thought, she launched herself at the door and bashed away at it with fists and feet. "Gods damn you! Open this door and talk to me! My people are bleeding and dying out on the trail! We need your help!"

Bennu put his arms around her and pulled her bodily away from the door. "Hold there, Ruia! Hold!" He was stronger than he looked. He half-carried, half-dragged her a few steps away. "Hold, damn you!" He adjusted his hold against her struggling and managed to get one arm around her neck, in a move that she vaguely remembered from her childhood wrestling bouts. She felt pressure on her neck, felt her breathing struggle, and forced herself to relax. Getting knocked out wasn't going to do her or her people any good.

She forced a few deep breaths into her lungs, and then slapped Bennu's arm several times. "All right, all right! Let me go."

He held her for another moment, then released her and took a few deep breaths of his own. "Gods, Ruia. You're wiry. Like an eel in the water. Gave this old man a bit of a run."

She stared at him, fuming. "If the captain can't help me, who can? My people don't have time for me to go to the governor's palace!"

He raised both hands in supplication to calm her, then indicated the letter in her hands. "May I see that letter?"

"Tjety said it was for the captain."

Bennu shook his head and spat toward the captain's closed door. "Our fearless captain is the worst kind of sand-dancer. He ain't gonna be any use to you, Ruia." He indicated the letter. "May I?"

She bit her lip, and even tried tapping into her *hekau* for some guidance. She didn't sense anything other than genuine curiosity and friendliness from Bennu. After another moment's thought, she handed it over, then draped Tjety's headcloth around her neck.

Bennu moved toward a long building set against the fort's plaster walls. "Come with me, Ruia. We'll get this sorted out, somehow." He nodded toward her. "And it looks like you could use something to eat."

She glanced at the captain's closed door again, sorely tempted to put a few bullets through it, just out of spite. She resisted, though, and followed Bennu, wondering if things would ever get any easier.

JETY BOUNCED ALONG IN the bed of the wagon, feeling the fever taking root deep within his body. Wounded villagers and children rode along with him while healthier folks jogged alongside the wagon, some with one hand on the wagon for support, the others just trotting along making the best time they could. The moon, the face of divine Khonsu, was high overhead in the cloud-filled sky, surrounded by countless stars. Trees lined the road on both sides, looming mysterious in the moonlight.

He occasionally found the strength to sit up and look along the path behind them, but it was hard to make out details between the low light and his fever-wracked sight. He would have made judicious use of his *hekau* to help detect anyone following them, but he was tapped out. The wound in his arm was a constant distraction, and he could feel the malignant heat within the wound creeping up and down his arm. The infection was spreading, and if he didn't get to a healer soon, he was going to die on this forsaken frontier.

Dwelling on the nearness of his eventual journey through the Duat, he had a sudden pang of guilt and longing for Heker. He was confident that it had been the right decision to have Ruia ride him to the fort as soon as possible, but he missed that horse. If he was going to die out here in the middle of nowhere, fighting for these people, he wanted to do it with his long-time friend with him. The thought of traveling the Duat without Heker was a frightening thing, and as he stared at the road passing behind them, he blinked hot tears out of his eyes.

One of the crones glanced at him. "You're leakin', Ranger. What do you see?"

He glanced at her and palmed away the tears with his good hand. What was he going to tell her? That he could see the deaths of all of them closing in, that they weren't going to make it to the fort? That they'd all be turned into those horrific unliving things, cheated out of any hope at a kind judgment?

No. He closed his eyes, took a deep breath, and found some vestige of inner peace. If his end was to be today, he'd go out with a fucking fight. He glanced at her.

"Just thinking about my horse. I miss that damn nag."

She snorted. "Well, that's a strange fuckin' thing to be thinking about at a time like this."

A rifle shot rang out just as he was about to offer a response. Setesk had stopped and fired at something behind them.

Tjety glanced down as the wagon rolled past the man. "What did you see?"

Setesk turned to jog alongside the wagon. "Maybe just a shadow, but I was sure I heard a horse."

Tjety focused on the road behind them and stared as hard as he could into the darkness. There might be forms out there moving through the trees and along the road, but it was just so damned hard to tell with the imperfect naked eye. He cursed himself again, wishing he had spent more time on his *hekau* studies. Master Waperineb would have been appalled at his student in the field.

Tjety shook off his doubts and glanced at Setesk.

"Hard to see anything. Best if you save your ammo for something more sure."

Setesk stared at him, then nodded. "I'll keep an eye out back here." He backed off from the wagon and lagged along behind.

Tjety took a breath to call out to the man, to encourage him to stick with the wagon, to not give himself up so easily, but no words came. He just didn't have the strength. He slumped back down into the bed of the wagon and dragged out his pistol and made sure it was loaded again. He knew he was stalling, but he needed something to do with his hand and his mind other than despair and doubt. He had five rounds left, and all of them were loaded in the pistol. The belt loops on his gun belt were all empty, something he hadn't had to deal with since training.

He glanced in the bed of the wagon. There were a handful of rifles and pistols taken from the bandits. If they got into a fight, they'd be able to last a little while, but at a guess he and the villagers had maybe fifty rounds among them. Definitely not much of an arsenal against an unknown number of enemy troops.

He wished he hadn't wasted the rounds on that

dark man, that he had engaged the man blade to blade, as that Zezago seemed to have wanted. But… no. He had no regrets. The Rangers were trained with the traditional forms of bladework, but more and more this modern world favored fast guns and hot ammunition. The old ways were falling by the wayside, along with the old empires. The new world was rising, one of steel and fire and big dreams bigger than national borders. He was alternately excited at the endless prospects and terrified to let go of the known world.

He snorted. He wouldn't have lasted long against Zezago with one fucking hand to fight with, anyway.

In spite of the bumping wagon, he drifted off, from exhaustion, from lack of food, from dwindling hope. He had a waking dream of staring out onto the wild frontier as a freak brushfire bit into the grasslands and swept over everything in its path, laying waste to all he could see from horizon to horizon.

Then, he saw himself reflected in a silvery pool of water, and his eyes changed from their dusky brown to a terrifying glowing emerald green. The flesh melted off his cheeks and his hair lengthened and turned gray. A grinning death's head wearing his

Ranger blue headcloth leered back at him, the glow from the green eyes searing into his *ba*. It opened its mouth and let out a blood-chilling yell.

Tjety snapped back to wakefulness as the driver of the wagon, Aniba, called out to him. "Wake up, Ranger! Something's happening!"

Tjety groggily blinked his eyes and stared around the wagon in confusion, his bearings slow to recover. A dozen pairs of frightened eyes stared back at him. He realized that the wagon was coming to a halt as Aniba called out to the horses to stop. Tjety reached out to the bench and hauled himself up to his knees, his legs and wounded arm screaming from the exertion. He glanced at Aniba. "Why have you stopped?"

Aniba pointed up into the sky. "Look!"

Tjety looked up into the star-dotted sky. A thin, bright red streamer of light soared up from a position ahead of them on the road, almost like a shooting star rising from the earth. It streaked high up into the sky and then suddenly exploded, bathing the ground all around in a flash of bright light.

In that moment of almost sun-like light, Tjety looked ahead and felt the blood in his face drain away. "Oh, shit."

Aniba glanced at him, then toward where he was looking, and echoed the curse.

A long line of those unliving creatures blocked the road to the fort. They were stretched from tree line to tree line, at least a dozen abreast, all with their green glowing eyes. They were profanity against the Lord Osiris and everything that Tjety held dear about life and death. The creature in the center of the group staggered a couple paces ahead of the line, and at some unheard command, the creatures started to shuffle toward the approaching wagon.

Tjety stared at the line of dead, certain that his premonition meant that he would join their ranks and soon. How could they fight such creatures?

A whooping noise behind them made him turn around. Shadowy forms on horses were moving in from the trees and the road behind them.

Oh, Lady Mayat. This was it, his last stand. His eyes felt as big as deben coins but a sudden spear of strength pierced his *ba* and shuddered up into his *hekau*. A mighty *djed* pillar wreathed in silver light flashed in his mind's eye, and he heard a simple command from his dread Lady Mayat.

"To the fort!"

She had spoken to him! By all the gods, she

had spoken! Inspired, he yelled out to the villagers milling around. "Come on! Get on the wagon!"

Tjety grabbed hands and arms and helped bodily drag the other survivors onto the wagon. He turned and slapped his hand down on Aniba's shoulder. "Drive, man, drive! Straight through that line!" He pointed toward the lurching creatures. "It's all we can do!"

A crazy jolt of hope crashed through his body, jerking his muscles to action. If they were going to die, they would go out in a white-hot blaze and take as many of those bastards as they could with them.

SERGEANT BENNU GUIDED RUIA to the long building set against the side of the fort wall and reached out to open the wooden door for her. A chorus of snores assaulted her ears, followed by the occasional grunt and a muttered request to close the fucking door and stop letting in the damn light.

Bennu gestured for her to enter. She walked into a lamp-lit bunkhouse, lined with twenty double bunks, most of which were filled with sleeping forms. Many of the soldiers had raw woolen blankets pulled over them, though a couple were laying naked on their bunks, their blankets fallen to the dirt flooring. She averted her eyes from the handful of naked and sleeping men and women.

Bennu indicated she take a seat at one of the

low tables set against one of the building's long walls. Cushions had been set on the floor, and she reluctantly sank down onto one, tucking her legs underneath her.

A sleepy voice sounded from one of the bunks. "A little young, ain't she, Bennu? Thought you liked them older."

Bennu glanced into the deeper darkness beyond the candles on the table. "Shut up, you, and get some sleep. We have ourselves a guest tonight."

The other voice muttered something she couldn't make out but suspected was rather rude.

Bennu grabbed an empty mug off the top of a cask, stuck it under the wooden tap, and filled it about halfway with a dark brew. He walked it over to Ruia and placed it on the table in front of her, then grabbed a half-loaf of bread thick with seeds out of a basket and broke it in his hands as he sat down.

"Here's a little beer and bread for you. I'll get the cook to work up some cold pork for you shortly." He indicated that she should eat and drink, and numbly, she did so, not sure what else do to.

She took a deep draught from the beer and coughed. It was much stronger than she was used to, even stronger than the stuff they had appropriated from the bandit's camp. She gnawed at the bread heel, finding that it tasted like rosemary and another herb she couldn't place. She nodded appreciatively as she ate. "Thank you for the bread."

He nodded and fished around behind him in another basket for a handful of figs. A couple looked to be on the edge of turning, so she picked out the best of the lot from his hand and nibbled around the edges, savoring the sweetness of it in her mouth compared to the bread and beer.

Bennu opened Tjety's letter and tipped it toward the candlelight, silently mouthing the words as he read. He chewed thoughtfully on another fig. "Cultists of Apep attacked your village?"

She heard the confusion in his voice. She glanced at him and then swallowed the bite of fig in her mouth. "Bandits, one-eared, with pistols and rifles. They also had...things with them, like justified dead pulled from their graves. Their eyes glowed green." She continued, alternating her story with drinking the beer and eating bread and figs. "They attacked during the day. Right out in the open under the bright watching eye of Re. They had guns and horses, and those unliving creatures..."

She took a breath, reliving the horror of the

attack. "We had a few guns in the village, but they weren't enough. I saw my da get hit and go down, and then my ma and the other elders. And there was so much blood. And the screaming."

She closed her eyes, clenching the scrap of bread in her hand. She reached up with her other hand and clasped her amulet, trying to find some peace from its soft pulses. "So many dead. I tried to fight, but one of those things hit me, and then there was a bandit with a rifle, and he hit me hard on the head."

She shivered, yet felt a calming through her *hekau*. "I woke up in a wagon with the other children from the village."

She focused on Bennu, and saw that several of the other soldiers had gotten out of their bunks and donned kilts or blankets and had joined them around the table. She drained the mug of beer. "There's maybe twenty of us left now, plus the Ranger, and they're all coming here, but I don't know how soon they'll get here, and I don't know if they're in trouble." She fought back the tears threatening to leak out of her again. "I don't have anywhere else to go."

Bennu shook his head. "And that damn captain, so afraid of his own shadow that he's not willing to lift a finger to help." He glanced at the other soldiers gathered around. "This ain't how we're supposed to defend the frontier for the pharaoh. If we're ever gonna take back our land and push the Hesso out, we're gonna need the villages in the province to support us, for supplies, if nothing else. Leaving them undefended is piss-poor policy."

Muttered agreements sounded through the room. Bennu dropped Tjety's letter on the table. "This here is a travesty of military proportion. And our captain ain't gonna do shit to protect anything except his own position." He banged a hand against the table. "He has conflicting orders from the governor and a mandate to do nothing but patrol areas that don't need to be patrolled." He focused on Ruia. "We should be riding out to escort your people back here, and then figure out what to do with them."

"But you're not. Is there anything you can do?"

Bennu glanced at the other troops. "Technically, no. When the captain tells us to do something or not do something, we have to follow those orders."

She glanced at him and then the other troops. "What if I asked for your help?" She stood up and glanced at each of them in turn. "The survivors of my village are out there somewhere, along with a wounded Ranger of Mayat. They're all tired, hungry, and hurt. They're riding in the dark. Can you help me guide them here?"

The soldiers traded looks with each other and with Bennu and started grumbling. Bennu raised his hands. "Now, you all listen to me and listen good. The reason we have this here captain is because we run out the last one that was in charge of this fort." He glanced at Ruia. "The last captain, may the gods rot his soul, was in the pocket of the Hesso. We didn't figure it out until it was almost too late, but we managed."

Ruia looked confused. "What happened?"

He shook his head. "To make a much too long story shorter, he led a column of men out to the Dunes and left them there, and came back here smooth as you please and told us they were doing the gods' work. That didn't sit well with the rest of us, so after finding out that all those troops had been killed out there, we put the captain in the stockade and forced the provincial governor to come here and resolve the situation."

Ruia frowned. "And?"

Bennu shrugged. "The coward sent his scribe and his son. The scribe took our report and handed us an execution order for the captain. After we'd taken care of that, the governor's son introduced himself as the new captain, and then took command of the fort and promptly locked himself in his quarters." Bennu shook his head, the disgust evident on his face. "Damn fool spends most of his time in there or in the senet house with the whores."

Ruia made a face at that. Bennu opened his mouth to add something, but before he could do so, the door to the barracks banged open and the gate guard rushed in. "Sergeant? Sergeant Bennu!"

Bennu glanced from Ruia to the guard. "What is it?"

The guard pointed out the open door. "In the sky! Some sort of light!"

Bennu was on his feet faster than his old bulk would have suggested he was capable of. He glanced out the door, turned his eyes skyward toward a bright, almost too-bright glow, and then glanced at Ruia. "Did the Ranger have a signal sparker?"

She shook her head as she approached the doorway herself. In the sky to the south of the fort, a dozen or more glowing fragments arced down toward the ground. She guessed they had originally been brighter, but as they fell, they gradually cooled and dimmed, winking out one by one until she could no longer see them beyond the buildings and the walls of the fort.

She stared up into Bennu's face. "What does it mean?"

"It means I go talk to the captain, and I mean right now." He glanced down at her and then at the other soldiers. "Get your gear together and help Ruia with her horse. I'll be back in a few minutes."

Ruia stood up. "I'm going with you, Bennu. I want some answers from that captain."

He glanced at her and patted her on the shoulder. "I don't think that's the best idea, Ruia." He indicated the pistol slung across her chest. "I'd fear you doing something rash." He raised his hands in front of her. "No, Ruia. Please, go with the soldiers and get your horse ready. We'll ride out together and find your people and the Ranger." He offered her a slight smile. "Trust me, Ruia."

She bit her lip, then nodded, feeling a twinge of strength ripple through her *hekau*, and maybe just the slightest whisper of confidence from some other, maybe even the Lady Mayat herself.

She watched Bennu leave the barracks, and then glanced at the gate guard, who shrugged then smiled. The troops started to file past her and out the door. One of the woman troopers leaned down and offered her hand. "Come on, Ruia. Let's get you to your horse."

Ruia reached out for her hand and let herself be pulled out of the barracks and toward the stables, her feelings a mix of dread from what the signal flare might have meant and hope for whatever Bennu and the other troops might be able to do to help.

16

ANIBA SLAPPED THE REINS of the horses over and over, charging them forward with fear in their cries. The dreadful line of creatures ahead drew closer in the night.

Tjety reached for another villager on the ground as the wagon lurched, but lost his footing and fell into the bed of the wagon. He managed to get back up to his knees, but the man had been left behind. He picked himself up off the ground and turned, aiming his rifle at the riders crowding down the road toward him. He managed to pick off one and shoot another's horse before he was shot down.

Tjety drew his pistol and braced his arm as best he could against the back of the wagon. He aimed at the approaching riders, and squeezed off a shot that just missed one of them. The bandit jerked his reins and started zagging toward the wagon, breaking up Tjety's hopes at getting a bead on him. Other villagers added gunfire to the melee. Bullets from the bandits whined all around and banged into the wood of the wagon.

Tjety glanced forward and quailed at the sight ahead. Those lumbering creatures were closing fast. He called out to Aniba. "Faster, faster! Work those nags for all they're worth!"

He suspected he'd have to answer to the gods for treating the poor beasts so harshly, but for now, people's lives mattered more than the horses. If they made it to the fort at the expense of two horses, he'd donate a year's salary to Pharaoh's fucking horse breeding program.

A couple of the villagers cried out at the sight ahead and switched their aim from the bandits behind them to the creatures ahead. More gunfire erupted, the bed of the wagon filling with expended shells from the rifles and the cries of the children and wounded. Gheti had found a pistol somewhere and fired it empty and then threw the thing toward one of the bandits, ululating a wicked cry all the while.

Tjety fired his pistol over and over, and then somewhere along the way realized he was dry-firing and holstered it in reflex. He leaned down and blindly scrabbled around in the bed of the wagon, as bits of wood splinters flew this way and that. One villager went spinning down to the bed of the wagon. Another was shot in the face and tumbled off the wagon. Reaching hands tried to grab at her but she was gone, lost in the tumult of raging hooves and the darkness.

"Ranger! Hold on tight! We're going through!"

Tjety had time to look ahead as the wagon closed in on the ragged line of unliving creatures ahead, and then held on for all he was worth as the horses screamed. They plowed into the ranks of the unliving, scattering bodies and parts of bodies every which way. As the horses and wagon plowed a deadly furrow, he saw a growing glow ahead. Fort Sekhmet with its torches lit up, the pylons and gates glowing in the moonlight like a beacon of hope. They were so close!

The wagon lurched, and he looked ahead to see the two horses faltering. One was heavily favoring one leg and both were covered in white foamy sweat and spittle. They were heaving hard, and if he'd been a more merciful man, he would have put them both out of their misery then and there. The brave animals were giving all they had left. He prayed to Mayat that they'd get them just a little further.

A bullet whined off the bench next to him and caught Aniba on the ricochet. He twisted on the bench and reached with both hands around to his back, dropping the reins that soon fell off the bench and got tangled up underneath the wagon. Tjety just missed grabbing them, but then grabbed hold of Aniba to keep him from falling off the wagon. They were a runaway now.

The horses surged forward on the road, clearly with no other thought in their minds than to run. Tjety lurched backward and fell into the bed of the wagon again, this time with Aniba in his arms. He cracked his head against someone or something in the wagon. Stars glittered in his vision.

One of the wagon wheels made a frightening popping sound, and then started to split. Tjety stared at it as the stars in his eyes faded. Time seemed to slow. The wheel disintegrated before his eyes, and then came apart completely.

The back left corner of the wagon sagged toward the ground and bounced heavily, jerking everyone in the bed of the wagon and leaving everyone to scramble for something to hold onto for dear life. Tjety flailed around with his good hand for something, anything to grab onto.

The wagon lurched again. Tjety looked behind the collapsing wagon. Several bandits still rode horses and a number of those creatures ambled toward the wagon, closing the distance now that the wagon was coming apart. He saw no sign of the dark man.

Then there was a great wrenching underneath his back and he bounced on the bed of the wagon once, twice, and then was thrown into the air. He landed hard on someone, rolled a few times, and plowed to a stop as bodies, parts of the wagon, and dirt fell all around him and on him. The stars in his vision returned, rivaling the numbers glowing in the sky overhead.

He blinked, shook his head, blinked again. Were the stars in his eyes or in his head? He couldn't be sure. His ears filled with roars, punctuated by ripples of sound that gradually coalesced into gunshots whining this way and that. He was on his feet one moment, then his knees, then back to his feet. The world spun around him as bullets whizzed by. He saw one of the boys, Henturu, maybe, sprawled out on the ground, and dragged him up into his arms. He staggered toward the fort, then fell over. He was just so tired. He was powerless to move, *hekau* spent, no bullets, out of time. Hopeless.

A sound somewhere nearby made him turn his head. Blurry objects moved into view, closing in on him. A cry sounded from somewhere and he managed to push his body over. That simple movement brought in a dark tunnel to his vision and he started to lose sight of where and when he was.

Something in front of him, something big. The wagon? No. The fort. The fort gate. The fort gate that now split open and revealed a bright vertical line of light—torchlight from inside.

The gates opened wide, and a dozen or more mounted soldiers thundered out, rushing toward him and the enemy somewhere around him. Near the center of the cluster of riders was Ruia, astride his beloved Heker, with a pistol in her hands and his blue headcloth tied around her neck, the ends of it billowing out behind her like a banner of hope.

17

THE SOLDIERS WITH RUIA led her first to the fort's armory, where they strapped on their greaves and bracers, and grabbed pistols and rifles and satchels full of bullets. She was encouraged to replace the old pistol hanging around her neck for a newer model, and one of the soldiers pressed an ammunition satchel into her hands. Caught in the whirlwind of activity, it was all she could do to maintain some level of focus.

She broke open the pistol after one of the soldiers showed her how, then loaded the thing with six rounds from her satchel. She closed it, then cocked and uncocked it several times to get the feel for it.

One of the soldiers glanced at her. "Happy?"

Ruia shrugged. "I guess so. I've only ever shot a pistol a few times. I don't know what I should be looking for."

Another soldier, a tall, dark-skinned man, grinned as he loaded shells into a shotgun. In a thick Hesso accent, he said, "Look for your foes. Shoots 'em before they shoots you." Another soldier clapped the Hesso on the back.

"Thanks, I guess." She straightened the holster sling around her chest and shoved her new pistol into it, and then slung the satchel over her neck and laid it cross-wise over her chest. She followed the now-armed soldiers outside, where Sergeant Bennu and some other soldiers were pulling horses together and tacking them up.

One soldier led Heker over to her. She was relieved to see him. She took the reins as the soldier grinned. "This is a damn fine horse, but he looks to be pretty well used up. Want a fresh mount?"

She shook her head. "He's come this far. I wouldn't want him to miss out on returning to his rider."

Someone must have uttered a command she didn't hear, because, as a unit, the men and women soldiers around her mounted up, all riding bareback in the Kekhmetic fashion. She did likewise, tamping down the combined jolts of fear and excitement coursing through her. She reached for her amulet and offered a quiet prayer to her mother and to the Lady Mayat then dug down into her *hekau* for some comfort and calm. The amulet pulsed softly in her hand, and she felt a gentle pull from deep within her *ba*, settling her nerves and adding some strength to her courage.

Distant sounds of gunfire and the screams of people and horses filtered in through the walls, breaking the stillness of the night. All the soldiers started and glanced at each other, some shooting looks toward Ruia. Gods. Those had to be her people out there, fighting to get to the fort!

"All right, this is it!" Bennu took his reins in hand and circled his horse, getting the attention of the troops arrayed around him. "The captain gave me a few troops. We ride out hard and look for any survivors of Ruia's company. Kill anything that looks like it needs to be killed. Any survivors, grab them— ride double or triple if you can—and get back to the safety behind the fort gates."

Several shouts of encouragement went up after that, and then Bennu heeled his horse over to Ruia.

"You ride next to me and stay close. We'll look for this Ranger of yours and bring him in, yes?"

She looked up at him, the hope surging in her soul. She drew her pistol, tightened Tjety's headcloth around her neck, and nodded. "I'm ready." The sounds of the battle outside the fort sounded ferocious, and she was alternately terrified and thrilled to be joining in the fray.

Bennu turned. "Open the gate and stand ready to repulse invaders. Now!"

The men at the locks moved the bars and swung open the gates. As soon as the space between the two gates was wide enough, Bennu heeled his horse and led Ruia and the others out of the fort, their collective hooves a thunder on the ground.

She rode out hard, managing to keep up with Bennu and the other soldiers. Heker seemed eager to ride into battle. Outside the fort was a long flat plain of tall grass, a dense treeline all around the edges of the grass. There was one road leading from the fort, and they followed that, toward where they had seen the signal light flash in the sky.

In short order, she saw the chaos of the battlefield. Her heart seemed to skip a beat. Those horrible mummified creatures were everywhere, attacking and chasing the villagers, some getting shot apart, some pummeling people on the ground with their moldering arms and fists. Bandits on horseback and some on the ground battled her people as well, using pistols, rifles, and knives seemingly at random.

The remains of the wagon were along the road, the two horses silent and still, tangled together in the leads and each other's limbs. Blood was everywhere. Several bodies lay around the wagon. As she focused in the darkness, she saw Tjety laid out near the wreckage, the unmoving form of little Henturu cradled close.

She shouted at Bennu and pointed toward what was left of the wagon. "There! The Ranger is there!"

Bennu glanced in that direction, nodded, and then pushed his horse that way. He called out, "Form a perimeter around the wagon! Rally there! Keep those bastards away from the survivors!"

Ruia rode alongside Bennu, and watched in wonder as the other soldiers efficiently maneuvered their horses into a rough circle around the wagon, dropping bandit and creature alike with well-aimed shots from the backs of their horses. Many of the soldiers may have looked young to her, but they seemed to be well-trained.

Bennu led Ruia into the center of the circle and gestured toward Tjety, who had slumped up against the wagon with Henturu in his arms. "See to him, Ruia! We'll cover you!" He waved to the other surviving villagers. "Get to a horse and rider! We all ride double back to the fort!"

Ruia leaped off Heker's back once she was close to the wagon and hurried over, skinning both knees as she hit the ground next to him and Henturu. Pain shot up both her legs, but she barely noticed in the rush. She shook Tjety, calling out his name. She could feel the heat pouring off of him, the fever clearly having taken hold. She didn't see any new wounds on his body, though he was so blood-stained and filthy that it was hard to tell. His pistol was in his holster and his khopesh was in its scabbard.

She also checked Henturu, relieved to see that he was still breathing. He had an ugly bruise on his head and a long, shallow gash across his chest. She looked around the battlefield and called out to Bennu. "Help, I need help! I can't get them both onto my horse!"

One of the soldiers in the defensive circle heard her and rode over, then dismounted to help, but was shot down by a bandit's cruel aim. Another soldier cut him down but was in turn shot in the back by another bandit and then trampled by one of the unliving creatures.

Ruia ducked as a fresh spatter of bullets crashed into the remains of the wagon all around her, and she drew her pistol and tried to shield both Henturu and Tjety with her body.

A third soldier and Bennu rode hard toward her, their rifles cracking in the air. More screams and cries sounded, and then there was a massive unliving beast looming ahead, its cruel glowing eyes focused on her. She raised her pistol and cried out as she squeezed the trigger over and over, sending pieces of it flying before scoring a hit in the center of its chest. Its heart-scarab exploded in a burst of green energy and limestone shards. The thing collapsed at her feet as Bennu rushed over on foot and bashed its head in with his rifle butt. Bits of bone and dessicated flesh burst into the air.

Bennu reached down and helped her to her feet, and then pulled Tjety up onto his shoulder. He yelled at her, "Get the boy and get on your horse! We have to get back to the fort!"

Ruia nodded, and somehow had the presence of mind to check her pistol. One unused bullet was still in it, so she broke it open and hurriedly replaced the spent cartridges with fresh ones from her satchel, but her hands were shaking so bad she dropped a few shells on the ground.

A yell from someone made her flinch, and she glanced and fired instinctively at a bandit streaking past on his horse. She didn't look to see if she hit him. She grabbed Henturu and half-dragged him over to Heker, where she bodily pushed him up onto the horse's back and then leaped up onto Heker. She scrabbled for the reins one-handed, then ducked as she sensed another rifle shot passing by. She felt a flare from her *hekau*, uncertain where the warning had come from.

She spared a glance for Bennu, who had slung Tjety onto his horse's back in front of him, and then started moving toward the fort gates. Several horses, loaded down with soldiers and village survivors, were making their way to the fort, though there were a few soldiers and horses down on the ground, and more villagers than she wanted to see wounded or dead.

To have fought for so long and to have died so close to the fort…

She shook off the despair that tried to grip at her

heart and dug deep into her *hekau*, which felt like a deep wellspring of strength. With new resolve, she turned toward the gates behind Bennu, riding Heker as hard as she dared.

A bandit desperately charged toward her from the edges of the perimeter. She cried out as she raised her pistol to shoot. In a surge of motion and a flare from her *hekau*, she held the reins and Henturu firm with one hand while she worked the deadly pistol with the other. With a steel grip and a deadly eye she never imagined possessing, she shot the man twice. He tumbled out of his saddle and onto the hard ground.

She barely registered what she had done as she galloped toward the gate, other soldiers and villagers filing in along with her. She reached the safety of the gates, and handed Henturu off to a soldier. Steady gunfire erupted from the walls of the fort. She glanced up. Several soldiers were set up along the walls with rifles, adding their deadly fire to the carnage.

Bennu rode up to her with a dark grin. "We've got most of the survivors in behind the walls, including your Ranger. I'm riding out to see if there are any more to pick up. Want to join me?"

She stared at him and realized dully that her hands were shaking, one on the reins, the other a vise on the pistol. He noticed and nodded, his expression turning somber. "I got the shakes too, the first time." He heeled his horse in close and rested a hand on hers, helping her pistol hand to stop shaking so badly. "Stay here. You've done enough for one day. You've done plenty, Ruia, and a damned fine job of it, too."

She stared at him as the tension in her body started to eat at her willpower, her ability to hold back the flood of emotions faltering. She forced herself to breath slow, then found the strength to holster the pistol, now a frightening thing in her hand.

Bennu nodded to her, then waved to a few of his allies and rode out through the gates.

Seated on Heker's back, Ruia stared around the interior of the fort. Soldiers guided her people toward the barracks. Someone called out her name, and then again when she didn't respond.

A form moved toward her out of the darkness, and grasped her leg. She looked down and saw Setesk, scratched and bloodied, holding a thick wad of bloodstained linen to his left eye. Now what?

He looked up at her with a stunned look on his

face. "Ruia! You got us to the fort, just as you said you would." He held her gaze and then grinned. "Didn't think you could do it, but we made it!" He seemed to realize he was holding onto her, and let go of her leg and stepped back. He shrugged, then said, "I…I guess I'm sorry for what I said and done earlier."

She was at a loss for words. She managed a weak smile and a nod. "It's enough that we made it, Setesk."

She nodded, mostly to herself, and then leaned over and rested her cheek against Heker's warm, heaving neck. "Praise and thanks to all the gentle gods, we made it."

ROM THE TREE LINE bordering the plain outside the fort, Zezago watched as the last stragglers from the fort's regiment trickled into the fort's gates. The gates closed behind the last man, blocking off access to the town beyond. The last few constructs staggered toward the fort's gates and walls, absorbing bullet after bullet hammered into them by the soldiers arrayed along the top of the fort's palisade wall.

Some of the constructs fell before reaching the gate, from either taking too much damage or from having their heart scarab blown apart. A couple actually reached the gates, but could do little more than pathetically claw at the unmoving structure before being shot to pieces.

He watched from the cover of the treeline, and

learned. Once he had ridden out onto the plain with his troops, he'd seen that the battle had already been lost. They were too close to the fort. He had moved to the treeline to study the battle, evaluating the soldiers but focused especially on the fall of that Ranger and then his subsequent rescue by that most curious villager girl. She'd ridden out of the fort along with several soldiers, and he was confident he caught the flare of *hekau* about her. If he had the opportunity, he would get a much closer look at her.

His constructs, though, their loss was frustrating. He already knew he'd have to work on a new batch, and would need to develop more varieties of scarabs. That would take time and effort, and more slaves. He studied the troops along the fort wall for a while longer, then slipped into the shadows of the trees.

In a small clearing, the ever-present and erstwhile Qebsenuf had gathered up the remains of his command and had the troops working on cleaning their weapons and getting their horses ready to hit the trail back to the quarry. He looked tired and worn down, but seemed to be the spot of calm in the storm of industry.

Zezago approached his lieutenant. "Well met, Qebsenuf. I see you survived the battle."

Qebsenuf offered a deferential bow. "Master Deshi. I am pleased to see you are also well." He glanced at his troops then smiled. "We fought hard, but numbers weren't on our side today."

Zezago found a seat on a tree stump. "Indeed. The Ranger did a masterful job of conducting an extended running fight where attrition proved to be our undoing. He and his cohort were able to whittle down our numbers faster than we were able to slow them down. And they managed to get close enough to the fort to benefit from those troops helping them as well."

Qebsenuf frowned. "Too true. Had we more men, or more constructs…"

Zezago raised a hand. "No, no. There is no reason for regrets or recriminations. We didn't have the volume of force we needed to take this day." He offered Qebsenuf a slow grin. "However, we have something that they do not have inside that fort."

Qebsenuf met his eyes, the puzzle in his mind clearly evident on his face. "And that is?"

Zezago's grin widened. "The casualties, of course. We have the raw material we need to start building another cadre of constructs right here before us."

Awareness dawned in his lieutenant's eyes. "Ah,

of course. We may not have a lot of living soldiers, but all the casualties on the field can be converted into more constructs."

Zezago stood and stretched his sore back, and stifled a cough before taking a deep breath. "Correct. We lost nearly twenty men today and more constructs besides. There are also the fallen troops from the fort and the dead villagers on the field. So many bodies. We'll take them all back to the quarry and convert them into constructs and then put them to work."

"We'd better work fast, then, before the sunrise." Qebsenuf waved over one of his sergeants. "Gather up a detail and start clearing the field of bodies. See if you can get that wagon fixed up enough for our use."

The sergeant bowed low to Qebsenuf, turned fearful eyes on Zezago, and then rushed off.

Zezago removed his headcloth and used it to wipe the sweat from his brow, then neatened it up and wrapped it around his head in neat, orderly folds. "Once that's done, gather up the men and make the best time you can back to the quarry. Get the construct process started on the new bodies and make sure the thralls still in camp are working as hard as they can. Now is not the time to ease off production. We have too much to do."

Qebsenuf gathered up his gear. "May I ask where you'll be in the meantime?"

Zezago signaled for an aide to bring him his horse. "Of course. I have some business to attend in the ruins of the temple beyond the fort. It'll take me some time to complete. Through tomorrow night and perhaps part of the following day."

Qebsenuf frowned. "We have a couple scouts left in the company. I could have them scout the fort…"

Zezago interrupted him with a shake of his head. "No, this requires my personal attention. There are things I need to evaluate, and it's best that I handle them personally." He looked in the direction of the fort, then returned his gaze to his lieutenant. "So you're aware of the larger picture, I intend to rebuild our company and then, when the timing is right, we're going to assault that fort and town and burn them to the ground."

Qebsenuf's eyebrows rose up. "We're going to attack the fort?"

Zezago nodded. "There are things I need in that ruined sun temple, and the fort and her population are in my way. Anyone we take alive we'll bend to our needs, and anyone that dies in the process, well… we'll put them to use as well, won't we?"

Qebsenuf furrowed his brow. "Of course, sir. You know I'll be wherever you need me to be."

Zezago nodded again, seeing his lieutenant in a new light. The man was flawed, but he was loyal and damned good at his job. Out here on the frontier, those were qualities in short supply.

Zezago offered his hand to Qebsenuf, who after a moment's hesitation, reached out and clasped it. "You're a fine lieutenant, Qebsenuf, and while I am not regular with my praise, know that I value your being here and I am grateful to have you leading my operation and my troops."

The look of wonder on Qebsenuf's face would have been touching had he been able to be touched, but it was encouraging to see all the same. "I live to serve, Master Deshi. Lead, and I will follow."

Zezago met Qebsenuf's eyes and felt vaguely uncomfortable, and was relieved to see the aide moving toward him with his mare in tow. Zezago accepted the reins and mounted Kubela, settling into the saddle. It'd been some time since he had ridden consistently, and his body was still sore from the day's riding.

He offered Qebsenuf a brief salute. "I leave the company in your charge, Qebsenuf. Get them home and get them working. I'll return soon. Don't wait for me."

Qebsenuf bowed low. "It will be done, Master Deshi. May your efforts prove worthwhile and may the mighty Apep protect you in his embrace."

Zezago nodded, then heeled Kubela toward the northern end of the treeline, leaving his lieutenant and company behind.

As he rode away, he began marshaling his *hekau*, setting up reserves to tap into later. He ruffled the tuft of mane between Kubela's ears. "I have plans within plans to enact, some traps to set, and triggers to pull. I'll need all the resources at my disposal to complete them." He stared toward the fort, and then nodded.

"That Ranger and his allies may have stolen victory from this battle, but the war is still very much anyone's for the winning." He patted the side of her neck. "And I intend to win."

The pieces he needed were moving into place, needing only a nudge here and there. And it would be he who would nudge those pieces and secure victory for himself and his House.

The adventures of Tjety and Ruia continue in
Pistols and Pyramids #3:

★

HOUSE
OF THE
HEALER

★

AFTERWORD

Thanks so much for picking up this book and trying it out. This weird blend of ancient Egypt and the American West is starting to grow on me, and I'm having a lot of fun researching both elements and finding new and interesting ways to twine them together. I hope you enjoyed reading it as much as I did writing it.

Honest book reviews are critical for writers; please consider leaving one on Amazon.com or wherever you purchased the book. If you'd like to learn more about Pistols and Pyramids and be first in line to hear news on my other writing projects and to get freebies and other goodies, sign up for my mailing list at www.scribeineti.com/newsletter. I send an email newsletter out about twice a month.

I love to hear from my readers, so feel free to drop me a note at jim@scribeineti.com and let me know what you think of the series and what your favorite Western movie or television show might be.

I trust you enjoyed your time in Kekhmet, and truly hope you'll return. May your horse be sound, your aim be true, and your scales be always in balance.

Jim Johnson
November 2015
Alexandria, VA

ACKNOWLEDGMENTS

As with the first episode, this book took a team to put together. This is my opportunity to thank that team. First, to my editor Erica Satifka, who provided critical commentary on the manuscript and whose efforts made this book and series far stronger. To my cover artist, print layout guru, friend, and fellow Literary Outlaw, Kevin G. Summers, who patiently worked with me through dozens of emails and Facebook conversations to get the cover text and layout just right. To my team of beta readers, thank you for your efforts. I didn't use all of your comments, but I hope I used the right ones. Your advice made this a better book and series.

Thanks to the members and participants of sundry online writing communities out there, including the Pulp Speeders, denizens of kboards' Writer's Cafe, the SFWA forums, and many others. I've learned from you all and have drawn inspiration from you all as well. Also, thanks to artist James Hale, who provided the illustrations you'll find in the print versions of these books. His sketches and final artwork provided a huge jolt of inspiration to my own humble *hekau*, fueling my desire to write these stories so that they lived up to his great artwork.

Special thanks to composers John Barry (*Dances With Wolves*), Jeff Beal (*Appaloosa*), Marco Beltrami (*3:10 to Yuma*), Bruce Broughton (*Tombstone*), Nick Cave & Warren Ellis (*The Assassination of Jesse James by the Coward Robert Ford*), Bill Elm and Woody Jackson (*Red Dead Redemption* and *Red Dead Redemption: Undead Nightmare*), James Newton Howard (*Wyatt Earp*), Kevin Kiner & Gustavo Santaolalla (*Hell on Wheels*), Ennio Morricone (too many to list), Lennie Niehaus (*Unforgiven*), Alan Silvestri (*The Quick and the Dead*), Keith Zizza (*Pharaoh, Children of the Nile)* and all of the musicians who worked with them on their respective scores and soundtracks. Your music was and is a constant inspiration during the development and writing of this series. Thank you all.

To my son Jacob Robert, who was born just a few weeks before I hit the 'Publish' button on the first book in this series: I love you, son. I sure hope you enjoy this series when you're old enough to read it.

And finally, to my wife Damaris: As always, thank

you for your love, your support, and your confidence in my efforts. I'm grateful you're with me on this crazy journey. Love you much, my dear.

ABOUT THE AUTHOR

Jim Johnson is the author of the *Pistols and Pyramids* series as well as other prose fiction series currently under development. He has written sundry other pieces of fiction, including several stories published in the *Star Trek* universe, and has freelanced for pen and paper roleplaying game companies, including Decipher and White Wolf. Please visit www.SCRIBEINETI.com for more information on Jim and his interests and writing.

When he is not busy writing and publishing and reading, Jim can be found catering to the Cat Overlords' collective demands; tinkering with LEGO brick creations; playing various console, board, and card games; contra dancing; playing djembe in a drum circle; listening to movie/television soundtracks and rap/hip-hop albums; and occasionally working with various community theater groups in the DC metro area. He may also be found catching a movie at the Alamo Drafthouse.

Jim lives in historic Alexandria, VA with his wife, newborn son, and several crazy cats.

The scales of justice are out of balance in Kekhmet. Follow the journey at:

WWW.PISTOLSANDPYRAMIDS.COM

THE SCALES ARE OUT OF BALANCE

PISTOLS & PYRAMIDS

EPISODE 1

★

RANGER
OF
MAYAT

★

JIM JOHNSON

THE SCALES ARE OUT OF BALANCE

PISTOLS & PYRAMIDS

EPISODE 2

★

FLIGHT
TO THE
FORT

★

JIM JOHNSON
AUTHOR OF RANGER OF MAYAT

THE SCALES ARE OUT OF BALANCE

PISTOLS & PYRAMIDS

EPISODE 3

★

HOUSE
OF THE
HEALER

★

JIM JOHNSON
AUTHOR OF RANGER OF MAYAT

THE SCALES ARE OUT OF BALANCE

PISTOLS & PYRAMIDS

EPISODE 4

★

THE
CURSED
SCARABS

★

JIM JOHNSON
AUTHOR OF RANGER OF MAYAT

MORE COMING SOON